PENGUIN BOOKS

A SUMMER BIRD-CAGE

Margaret Drabble was born in Sheffield in 1939 and went to the Mount School, York, a Quaker boarding school. She won a Major Scholarship to Newnham College, Cambridge, where she read English. She was awarded the CBE in 1980.

Her novels include: *A Summer Bird-Cage* (1963), *The Garrick Year* (1964), *The Millstone* (1965, filmed as *A Touch of Love* in 1969), *Jerusalem the Golden* (1967), *The Waterfall* (1969), *The Needle's Eye* (1972), *The Realms of Gold* (1975), *The Ice Age* (1977), *The Middle Ground* (1980), *The Radiant Way* (1987), *A Natural Curiosity* (1989) and *The Gates of Ivory* (1991), all of which have been published by Penguin. She has also published a short critical book on Wordsworth and many articles, as well as *Arnold Bennett: A Biography* (1974), *The Genius of Thomas Hardy* (1976, edited), *A Writer's Britain* (1979) and *The Oxford Companion to English Literature* (1985, edited).

Margaret Drabble is married to the biographer Michael Holroyd and lives in London.

Margaret Drabble

A Summer Bird-Cage

Penguin Books

PENGUIN BOOKS

Published by the Penguin Group
Penguin Books Ltd, 27 Wrights Lane, London W8 5TZ, England
Penguin Books USA Inc., 375 Hudson Street, New York, New York 10014, USA
Penguin Books Australia Ltd, Ringwood, Victoria, Australia
Penguin Books Canada Ltd, 10 Alcorn Avenue, Toronto, Ontario, Canada M4V 3B2
Penguin Books (NZ) Ltd, 182–190 Wairau Road, Auckland 10, New Zealand

Penguin Books Ltd, Registered Offices: Harmondsworth, Middlesex, England

First published by Weidenfeld & Nicolson 1963
Reprinted in Penguin Books 1967
20

Printed in England by Clays Ltd, St Ives plc
Set in Monotype Imprint

Contents

1   The Crossing   7

2   The Wedding   19

3   The Reception   35

4   The Move   53

5   The Invitation   73

6   The Party   80

7   The Next Invitation   99

8   The Next Party   115

9   The Information   134

10   The Convergence   153

11   The Collision   170

FOR CLIVE

'Tis just like a summer bird-cage in a garden:
the birds that are without despair to get
in, and the birds that are within despair and
are in a consumption for fear they shall never
get out.

John Webster

1 The Crossing

I had to come home for my sister's wedding. Home is a house in Warwickshire, and where I was coming from was Paris. I was keen on Paris, but will refrain from launching into descriptions of the Seine. I would if I could, but I can't. I like the way things look, but can never remember them when I need to. So I'll leave Paris at that. I was leaving to go home to be a bridesmaid at the wedding of my sister Louise. And I didn't mind leaving, either: all the foreignness that seemed so enchanting when I first went in July had begun to drive me to distraction. Every time somebody pinched me on the Métro I felt like screaming, and as for things like the lavatory paper and the price of chocolate and the brisk, bare-kneed, smart little girls I used to take for English conversation – well, I felt I'd really had enough. I'd only been there for two months, but it seemed like far longer. So when the letter arrived from Louise asking me to go and bridesmaid, I heaved a sigh of relief and bought my ticket. Also, I felt that it was time I stopped wasting time. I don't know why I hate wasting time so much.

I hadn't really been doing anything in Paris. I had gone there immediately after coming down from Oxford with a lovely, shiny, useless new degree, in a *faute-de-mieux* middle-class way, to fill in time. To fill in time till what? What indeed? It was quite pleasant, teaching those birdy girls, but it wasn't serious enough for me. It didn't get me anywhere. So when Louise wrote, the thought of England rose before me, gloomy, cold, but definitely serious. And as I wanted to be serious, I bought my ticket home, said goodbye to the girls and my landlady, and turned my thoughts to the Appointments Board, and National Insurance, and other such eminently serious subjects. I thought about them all the way to Calais, through the sandy flats, as I chewed a garlic-laden ham roll. I thought about jobs, and seriousness, and about what a girl can do with herself if over-educated and lacking a sense of vocation. Louise had one answer, of course. She was getting married. Moreover she was marrying a very wealthy and, in a minor way, celebrated man. It seemed to be one way of escaping the secretarial course-coffee bar degradation that had been creeping up on her ever since, two years ago, she too had left the esoteric masonic paradise of Oxford.

On the other hand I wouldn't have married Stephen Halifax had he been the last exit open to me. I didn't know why I disliked him so much: I wasn't even sure if what I felt was dislike. Perhaps it was partly fear. I was intimidated and inhibited by the fact that he was a novelist, with four novels to his credit, all of which had received rather flattering reviews. Success is always scaring, particularly to the ambitious. Also, I hated his books. They were horrible books, but good as well as horrible: if one hadn't known him one would have assumed that their author was sour, middle-aged and queer, whereas Stephen is sour, thirty, and married to my sister, whatever that may or may not mean. All four of them are full of social sneers and witty, thin-lipped observations. He never makes a joke. I dislike books without jokes. Even bad Victorian ones are better than nothing. I don't think Stephen likes jokes at all. The reviews say he is a social satirist, and talk about his delicate perception and keen wit, but for me they can keep them. He behaves like his books as well: when I talk to him, I always feel that I am badly dressed and have the wrong accent. I am sure

8

this is what he does think, but as he thinks the same about everyone, his opinion is hardly objective. Nobody escapes. Everyone is either ridiculously rich, or ridiculously poor, or ridiculously mediocre, or ridiculously classy. He leaves no possibility of being in the right, unless he means to leave himself as a standard, which would be logical, as he is almost entirely negative. He looks grey. It must be his skin, because his hair is a normal shade of brown. He looks very inconspicuous and distinguished and grey.

I couldn't imagine why Louise was marrying him. I knew she had been seeing quite a lot of him since she left Oxford and went to live in a flat off the Fulham Road, but I had never thought it would come to this. I could see that he was quite a nice sort of person to have dinner with from time to time, as one would be able to have all the expensive things on the menu, but as for marrying – and as for Louise marrying. My sister, I should say, is an absolutely knock-out beauty. She really is. People are silent when she enters rooms, they stare at her on buses, they look round as she walks down the street. I don't know where she gets it from. My mother is quite pretty, but in a twittering, soft sort of way, and so am I, I suppose, whereas Louise has a real old aristocratic predatory grandeur. As tags go, she is *grande dame* where I am *jeune fille*, and she leads all her life to match it. She has a very pale skin and fabulous eyebrows and black hair and a tall, stiletto sort of figure and so forth. I thought to myself, as the train went past all the back views of houses that mean Calais, that perhaps Stephen was marrying her because she never looked ridiculous. At the worst he could call her aquiline and intense, but even that sounds quite impressive. Perhaps he wanted a wife to be a figurehead to his triumphal car, a public admiring ornament to his house. A hostess. But I couldn't see what there was in that for her; she was never a great one for playing second fiddle. On the contrary, she was inclined to be ruthless about getting what she

9

wanted. I supposed it was possible that she wanted Stephen. It occurred to me as the train began to slow down that perhaps she was in love with Stephen, and then it occurred a second afterwards that since this was such an obvious explanation it would certainly have occurred earlier if true. So I discounted the concept of love.

At least with regard to old Louise. Love. Love. I thought idly of Martin who had bidden me farewell on the Gare du Nord at seven-thirty that morning. It was nice of him to have got up. I had been sorry to leave him, and we had both clung a bit, but not significantly. I was glad, really, that there was a certain amount of wrench involved in leaving. It made the fact that I was going seem more of a decision and less of a drift. I thought how much less impossible it was that I should marry Martin or almost anyone than it was that Louise should marry Stephen Halifax. What a name. Stephen Halifax. At least I would find out at this wedding whether it was a pseudonym or not. Louise said it wasn't but it didn't sound at all real to me.

The train stopped. With a rush I felt terribly sad about French trains and notices saying *Ne te penche pas au Dehors* (is that what they do say? *TE*? Why not *vous*?): and as immediately forgot my sadness in the wave of fury that overwhelms me during the pushing, banging, queueing and waiting that accompanies getting off the train, through the Customs and on to the boat. I never get a porter, mainly because I hate being parted from my luggage, and so suffer all the irritation of battered legs, aching arms and hair in my eyes with no hand free to push it out of the way. I don't know why I punish myself so, but I always do. I'm a menace on holidays or journeys, I can't enjoy myself unless I do everything the hard way. Perhaps I do it on purpose, because the feeling of relief and spaciousness that succeeds sweaty exhaustion the minute one gets on the boat is wonderful and can only be savoured after undergoing the full initiation of effort. Nothing enchants me as much as the channel crossing. I hope they never make a tunnel. I've been across ten times now and each time I have been entranced and absorbed by everything, the harbour, the people, the inaudible announcements, the smell, the ladies' rooms, the bars with cheap cigarettes which I regret not wanting, and delicious chocolate. I buy French chocolate going out and English coming back. There is something so solid and homely about Cadbury's Milk in sixpenny blocks, and sixpence seems so extraordinarily little to pay for a whole bar.

I bought two and sat with them on the deck; it was a marvellous day, sunny and windy with lots of white clouds whipping across the sky. People kept being sick, which cheered me as I never am and I like feeling tougher than others. I sat and let the wind blow my hair about and remembered my last crossing which had been after a month in Italy and an unspeakable overnight journey on a students' train from Milan: apart from being totally unable to sleep or even doze off, I had also frozen to death as I had no coat of any sort with me, only a large jersey and thin cotton jeans, which, as the train rolled through the icy Alps and equally icy Strasbourg, *etcetera*, had proved alarmingly inadequate. In the end I had abandoned my seat and gone to sit in the corridor, where, by the dim light of passing stations and all-night factories, I read Plato's *Republic* on which I was due to write an essay the following week. On the boat Simon, who is somewhat of a *bon viveur* in a youthful way, had insisted that he and Kay and I should have a proper meal in the restaurant, and we had finished the chianti we had bought just before leaving Milan, and afterwards we sat below the deck, warm and sleepy, amongst a party of Chinese immigrants coming from God-knows-where. It had been charming, but it was also charming to sit alone in the wind eating chocolate and making eyes at passing men.

Folkestone looked so delightfully ugly when we arrived,

all the solid-fronted hotels and terrace houses. Oh, I felt so cheerful until I got on the train. I hate trains. I slept all the way to London, and woke up with a headache and a grudge against the whole journey. Honestly, I said to myself as I lugged my case along Charing Cross Station and on to a bus to Paddington, honestly, Louise is so selfish to drag me all the way home to this foul ugly country where people never smile at you or pinch your bottom in passing, where it rains all year round and the buildings are the most hideous in the world. I was really gloomy when I arrived at Paddington, especially as I found I had just missed a train, so I rang up home to inform them of my arrival without very much enthusiasm. When the 'phone was eventually picked up I said, 'Hello, this is Sarah, who's that?' and a cool voice said 'Louise.' Nothing else, nothing about how nice to have you home, just 'Louise.'

'Good heavens,' I said. 'How are you?'

'Fine. And you?'

'Fine too.'

'Where are you?'

'I'm at Paddington. I'll arrive at New Street at eight-five.'

'All right. Shall I come out and meet you?'

That really shook me. 'Oh, there's no need for that,' I said. 'I'm sure Daddy will if you ask him.'

'No, no, I'll do it. I wouldn't mind getting out for an hour.'

There was almost a gleam of expression in that last sentence, so I ventured on a question. 'How are things at home?' I asked.

She heaved a great sigh that rattled down the receiver. 'Oh, bloody,' she said. 'You know, people all over, presents, the hotel demanding numbers, letters to write, and old Daphne poking her nose in. She even comes into my bedroom,' said Louise, in tones of such disdain that she might have been talking about an earwig, not a first cousin.

'Never mind,' I said. 'You'll be out of it soon enough.'

'That's what I tell myself.'

'Is my dress there?'

'Oh yes.'

'I hope it fits.'

'It won't be my fault if it doesn't. I told you to come home earlier to have it fitted. And as for sending your measurements in centimetres, Miss McCabe was quite out of her depth.'

'There aren't any inches in Paris.'

'Oh well, never mind, you can't look worse than Daphne anyway, can you?'

'Oh, Louise.'

'Well, it's true.'

'Where are they all at the moment?'

'Having tea.'

'Oh, I see. Well, you'd better go and join them.'

'See you,' said Louise, and rang off. Not for her a diminuendo of 'Well, it's been nice hearing you, and you too, thank you for ringing, good-bye, good-bye, good-bye, 'bye then, see you, 'bye then,' off.

I went and bought myself an *Evening Standard* and got on the train, where I read it and *Tender is the Night* (beta minus) and watched the monotonous countryside enlivened only by the occasional ancient church-spire. I began to get gritty and sticky and confused in my mind, and to think petty niggling thoughts about bridesmaids' dresses and our ghastly cousin Daphne and why on earth Louise was getting married at home instead of in London. I mean to say, why have hundreds of guests and white veils and champagne in Warwickshire? There must have been some point of etiquette involved too subtle for me to understand: Louise is a great one for etiquette.

So, my mind thus nastily occupied, I arrived at New

Street, and stoically, irritably, heaved my cases down from the rack and carried them along the platform. I was just about to think 'Of course she isn't on time' when I caught sight of her, with her back to the train and platform, playing with one of those letter-punching machines. She seemed dozing and abstracted. The usual envy filled me as I took note of her beautifully pinned and coiled hair, the clear beige and neatness of her jersey, and the uncreased look of her linen trousers. I was wearing linen trousers too, but mine were of the baggy at the knee variety, and I suddenly felt shabby and travel-stained, reduced to a schoolgirl with twisted belt, mac down to ankles, and one plait undone. She always does that to me. Always. I put my cases down, pushed the hair out of my eyes, and said 'Hi, Loulou.'

She turned round and said, 'Oh, there you are.' Then she turned back to her machine and pushed the button. A metal tag came out. She looked at it and dropped it on the platform. I glanced down at it. It said LOUISE BENNETT XXXXXXXX.

'I wondered if I'd got the right train,' she said.

'You certainly had,' I said. 'It was a horrible train. Thank heaven that's over, I'm fed up with travelling.'

'Well, come on then,' she said. 'Let's get a porter.'

Unprotesting, I let her collect one, which she did with ease as all the available ones were gaping at her anyway. Then she ambled off like an heiress, and I shuffled behind like Cinderella or rather one of her ugly sisters after the pumpkin episode. Louise didn't say anything till we got to the car (I had to tip the porter with one of my last shillings); there, she switched on the engine, looked at herself in the driving mirror with that withdrawn narcissistic nonchalance she has, adjusted it, and said, 'Well, what was Paris like?'

I wished she could manage to sound just a little more interested.

'I don't know,' I said. 'Pretty marvellous really, I suppose.'

She drove off. She drives quite well, I think.

'I suppo e you associated with all those beatniks,' she said, after another long pause.

'Beatniks come from America,' I said. 'It's existentialists in Paris.'

'Still?'

'Why not?'

'Oh, I don't know.'

'Anyway, I didn't. I spent most of the time with some rather smart silly girls I was teaching, and a man called Martin who was working in a bookshop.' I thought back to Martin, and became expansive: I told her about how we used to meet for breakfast in the bar under my bed-sitter, and how he spoke such wonderful French that everyone thought he was, though he just learned it at school like everyone else, and about the day we went to Versailles and our train got stuck in a siding. I amused myself by recounting it, even though I didn't much amuse her. She gave very little in exchange – a few odd remarks about cousins Daphne and Michael and Aunt Betty, my mother's sad widowed sister, and about wedding presents. Not a word about Stephen. After a while we lapsed into silence.

I looked out of the window. The country looked so different from the car: it looked unique and beautiful, not flat and deadly. Once one gets through the industrial landscape, which I think very impressive and dignified, the rusticity is enchanting. It was getting towards dusk, and the autumnal colours were deeper and heavier in the sinking light: the fields of corn were a dark brown and gold, dotted ecstatically with poppies. I was moved by their intermingling tones. The sky was purplish, with breaks of light coming somehow closer in front of a sombre, solid background of clouds that looked like plush. Oh, it was beautiful, very much England and beautiful. Why aren't they enough, why won't they do, things like that, rainbows and cornfields.

I always enjoy arriving home however much I hate it when I get there. Hope certainly springs eternal in the human breast, and I think after every absence that my family will have improved, though it never does. A faint warm and cosy feeling overcame me as we drove up the drive and saw Mama, who had heard the car, standing at the doorway. She was so delighted to see me, so touched and excited by my arrival, that I caught her enthusiasm. She always liked me best. I despise myself at times for giving in to the bargain comfort of meals provided and beds made, but she sees nothing wrong in it all. She doesn't think it's weak to like being looked after, she thinks it's natural, she thinks I'm mad to prefer the dirt and weariness and loneliness that I am prepared to suffer in order to gain a sense of hope. It always takes me a day or two, though, to realize why there is no possibility in my home, and so I sat down that evening quite comfortably amid the faces and furniture of the drawing-room to eat my plate of cold chicken, and thought how pleasant and unobjectionable fitted carpets and curtains with pelmets and wall-lights like candles and chiming door-bells really are. I persuaded my father to open the bottle of liqueur I had brought for him, and we drank it with the coffee, and told anecdotes and listened to wedding problems and looked at wedding presents. I had brought them each something – the Cointreau for Papa, perfume for Mama and Aunt Betty and Daphne, five yellow-backed books for Louise and a tie for Michael, not chosen by me. He seemed to like it: it was the only thing I had had doubts about. Some of Louise's wedding presents were wonderful, blissful glass objects and hot-plates and silver. But she didn't seem very interested in them herself. She didn't seem concerned.

I like my cousin Michael. We are exactly the same age, to a couple of weeks, and we got on very well as children. Daphne is three years older, Louise's age, a plain bespectacled girl, now a schoolmistress, and one of those I imagine who bring despair to the hearts of young girls as they view the narrow grey horizons of maturity through such lenses. It had been one of my only holds over Louise in our early childhood, that Michael was my friend, not hers: when we went to stay with my aunt during my parents' too frequent holidays without us, I used to gain in stature and to expand, while Louise would retire irritably with a book and refuse to play with Daphne at all. I didn't realize then, though I do now, that she must have been very jealous of me and Michael; usually at home I was always pestering her to talk to me or to take me with her on expeditions, but at Aunt B's I had no need to trouble her. Indeed, part of my pleasure in playing with Michael was relief at not having to disturb Louise, who always used to snap at me or bully me or ignore me when I did: but in reality I suppose she missed my timid, obsequious attentions. Anyway, some of the old bond between Michael and me remained: he was a rugger boy, but of the very nicest type, and he and I had quite a talk about Paris, and he told me about his new girl. He said he was going to France himself next month and I thought I would give him Martin's address. And while we all talked and sipped our Cointreau and rejoiced in our smugness, Louise sat on the rose tapestry chair in the corner and wrote thank-you letters in her wild enormous handwriting at my mother's desk.

It was when I went to bed that I felt the biggest pull of the comfort thing. There is something so alluring about my own room that – after French beds and cigarette ends all over and wine on the counterpane – is utterly demoralizing. After undressing in front of an unnecessary gas fire, I wandered round opening drawers and looking at clothes I had forgotten and old letters, and myself in the large subservient mirrors. Then I got into bed, and as I lay there reading in the clean tight sheets in a spinsterish delight, I wondered why on earth I disliked being at home so much.

2 The Wedding

I found out, of course, in the morning. After the first glow of welcome came the usual nags, complaints, demands and grudges: my mother complained to me unendingly about Louise, about the guests she invited who never replied, about the way she left packing straw all over the hall, and about our Swedish girl Kristin: my father told me my mother was run down and that my place was at home and what did I mean by arriving only two days before the wedding: Daphne peered and chatted at me and told me heart-breaking, pathetic stories about the classics master at the Boys' Grammar School who apparently took her to the cinema from time to time. Louise ignored me and everyone else completely. Aunt Betty was as quiet and mournful as ever, uncomplaining and forbearing and worn to a shadow by her widowhood. She was everybody's stooge: everybody took it out of her. The whole set-up seemed so fossilized and gloomy that I decided that the gleams of goodwill had as ever been pure hallucination, and that I had better get out as soon after Louise had departed as possible. The only consolation was Michael, who walked with me round our rather Elizabethan garden, full of camomile and gillyflowers and pease-blossom, pulling flowers off plants in a way that drives Mama mad, and telling me what he thought of Stephen. What he thought wasn't much, as I had expected, but he said with enviable cynicism, 'Oh, she probably knows which side her bread is buttered.' Michael and I used to amuse ourselves by a little mild flirtation: although he was such an old acquaintance we were both well aware that we were more than relations and that the prayer-book said we could get married if we wanted. We didn't want, but it added a little incestuous spice to family life to think about the possibility. The year before he had even tried to kiss me, but I think we were both rather disgusted by the event, and had since confined ourselves to innuendo and accidentally brushing hands and provocative chat about other girls of his or men of mine.

With everybody else being in such a bad temper about one thing and another, I managed to hit the right note of irritation by getting really annoyed about my bridesmaid's dress. It was very smart, and it fitted perfectly, but I thought it was rather tarty, and was surprised at Louise until I remembered that she wasn't wearing it herself. Her dress was quite lovely, or seemed to be through its plastic bag in the cupboard; it was made of wild silk and was simple and floating. I knew she would look so extraordinary that I wished I could be generous and admire her just for a couple of days without grudging it. But she was so ungenerous herself that I couldn't. Until I went up to Oxford I always believed that the defensive, almost whining position that she invariably pushed me into was entirely the fault of my own miserable nature, as I admired her fanatically: it was only at university that I realized that it was she that forced me into grudgingness. In fact, I never realized this of my own accord at all: it was explained to me by a friend, and it took me a very long time to grasp the idea and to live with it. I always have birth-pangs over new ideas, prolonged sickness, head-aches and misery before the final painful delivery: but after that the idea is with me for ever, kicking and alive. I could never thank Peter enough for delivering this idea about Louise: his theory was, I think, essentially the right one, and it lifted a load of dependence and clinging inferiority from my shoulders. It was at Oxford that I began to forget her: I didn't think about her for whole days together: I didn't think people were being kind when they complimented me on my appearance. I was always a one for seeing things in extremes, and because I wasn't as beautiful as Louise I assumed I was as plain as Daphne: whereas in fact if there is a barrier down the middle of mankind dividing the sheep from the goats I am certainly on Louise's side of it as far as physical beauty goes.

It was a horrible day. A day of bad temper, and in me of age-old, cradle-born superfluity. A day of old feuds. The thought of Louise getting married the next day seemed to annoy everybody, including Louise. We all went to bed fairly early, wishing Louise a solemn good night: at dinner my mother had suddenly and unexpectedly turned senti-mental, reminiscing about her own honeymoon in a solitary unsupported monologue. I felt sorry for her as my father wouldn't cooperate at all: poor brave twittering Mama, pretending everything had always been so lovely, ignoring the facts because they were the only ones she knew. My father is a bit of a brute and that phrase really fits him; at such times he rudely and abruptly dissociates himself from everything Mama says, so she has no retreat except repellent Louise and soft, dishonest, indul-gent me. So I asked the right questions and listened to the old stories, which would have been charming if true, and went to bed feeling sick with myself and sick with the whole idea of marriage and sickest of all with Louise, who didn't even seem to realize the courage and desperation of Mama that underlaid the nonsense and fuss and chirruping.

I fell asleep quickly and was awakened at four in the morning by noises from downstairs. I lay there for a few minutes in a headaching bad temper wondering what on earth it was, until it occurred to me that it might well be Louise suffering from traditional bridal sleeplessness. I tried to get to sleep again, but couldn't, and after tossing and turning and switching the light on and off several times I decided to get up and investigate. I put on my dressing-gown – and crept to the top of the stairs: the hall light wasn't on, but the light in the music-room was, and I could see Louise walking firmly and regularly from one end of it, along the hall to the front door, and back again, backwards and forwards, like an animal in a small cage trying to take exercise. She had bare feet and was wearing a white nightgown that looked like part of a trousseau; it had a black ribbon threaded round the lace at the neck. There was something padding and rhythmic in her step that suggested she had been there for a long time, walking up and down. She was smoking and dropping cigarette ash on the floor as she went. I watched her make her short pilgrimage two or three times more before I said, 'Lou,' and she looked up as she reached the bottom of the stairs and saw me: 'Who's that?' she said, with a little giggle, and I said 'Sarah,' and she said, 'Oh, that's all right!' with a sigh of relief. Then, with the same subterranean giggle in her voice, she went on, 'Come on down then, come and join the party.'

She sounded very approachable, so I went down and we went into the music-room where the light was. She sat down on the settee, very heavily, and said, 'Look, Sally, I'm drinking in the dawn.' And she was too: she had half-finished a bottle of whisky: she handed it to me with a kind of bonhomie that was quite unprecedented, and said, 'Go on, have a drink.'

I obeyed, though the stuff tasted very sour and odd in my half-asleep mouth, and then I looked around. Everywhere was littered with ash, little grey worms of it all over the carpet, and Louise herself looked quite fantastic, her long hair all wild and tangled up with two odd curlers stuck in the top, and her skin glistening white and deathly with cold cream.

'What the hell do you think you are?' I said. 'Lady Macbeth?'

'How did you guess,' she said, 'how did you guess. And how did you know I was here?'

'I heard you. You woke me up.'

'Oh Christ, that must have been when I fell over the piano stool. I'm not really making a noise.'

'Oh no. And look at that ash.'

She looked at it, comically helpless.

'Yes, it is rather a mess, isn't it. What on earth can I do with it? And all that whisky. Could I fill it up with water, do you think?'

'Don't be silly, you'll be in Rome before it's discovered.'

'Yes, so I will. So I will. I keep forgetting.' She paused and belched. 'I say, Sally, I feel ghastly.'

'I'm sure you do,' I said, primly. 'Would you like me to make you some coffee?'

'Oh, Sarah, be an angel. I'd love some. I could just do with some. Do make me some, I need looking after for once in my life, I'm too weak to switch the gas on. Do be an angel, I'll love you for ever if you make me some coffee.'

I could have done with that too.

It was soft of me, I suppose, but I was so honoured by her drunken accessibility that I took her into the kitchen and sat her down at the table, made her some Nescafé, and swept up all the ash quietly with a dustpan and brush. Then she started to moan about her hair so I fetched the rest of her curlers and put it all up for her. She looked only faintly ridiculous even with her hair full of iron rolls and her face shining with grease: somehow she managed to look dramatic rather than at a disadvantage. She looked as though she were in a film or an air raid. She was more communicative than I had ever known her, and kept muttering about Rome and loving, honouring and obeying: she said nothing about Stephen except, 'Stephen knows such gorgeous people in Rome,' which came up from time to time as a refrain. I envied her, for her honeymoon if not for her husband, and told her so: 'I wouldn't mind larking about in first class hotels for a bit,' I said. She was pleased that I was impressed. After a while the blodginess and irritation of being up in the middle of the night left me, and I fell in with the isolated moment, the dark kitchen, Louise leaning on her elbows with her face in her hands, the smell of ash and cold cream, and the sudden disruption of twenty-one years of family life, during which I had never been up at that hour except when ill. Louise kept going on so about Rome that I too started to think of it: there is something about Italy that fills me with such desire: even the names are so incantatory that they put me under – Florence, Arno, Ferrara, Siena, Venice, Tintoretto, Cimabue, Orvieto, Lachrimae Christi permesso, limonata – just the sound of them reminds me that I am not all dry grit and deserted hollows. As Kingsley Amis might put it, I am a nut case about abroad. I love E. M. Forster for loving it: I love George Eliot for her monstrous dedicated ardour in *Romola*: I love those two lines of Keats which I first found used to illustrate some long-forgotten figure of speech in a grammar textbook –

> 'So the two brothers and their murdered man
> Rode past fair Florence.'

Fair Florence, with the sculpture and the water-ices. I gave myself up to the idea of it, I wallowed in nostalgia – stupidly, as I had only got back from abroad the day before and was due in fact for a spell of English Victoriana-worship – I envied Louise for going there the minute that trivial business of getting married was over. A honeymoon and Rome, what an *embarras de richesses*. I would have changed places in a flash, if only I could have chosen a different man. I could have made good use of those nice little stapled booklets of tickets.

I must say, in justice, that there was something so almost gay in the way Louise talked about those gorgeous people, and her trousseau, and the hotels, that I was quite prepared to believe that everything was perfectly normal and happy, and even that she might be in love: certainly that life would be beautiful and exciting and highly-coloured for her, which for other people may well be just as good as love. I did not think that the drabness and despair which threatened to ooze over my life in every unoccupied second would ever swamp Louise: she was way off, wealthy, up in the sky and singing. Louise, Louise, I mutely cried as we went up to bed for the last two hours of the night, Louise teach me how to win, teach me to be undefeated, teach me to trample without wincing. Teach me the art of discarding. Teach me success.

Her wedding morning was bright and promising. She got up earlier than usual, looking wax-coloured and stiff. She came down to breakfast, one of those lapsed middle-class events which she normally used to miss. This had been one of my mother's grievances, and I thought never again will she have that to complain about. We could never see what difference it made if we came down to breakfast or not, as we were quite prepared to fast if we got up late. But mother didn't see it that way. Our domestic help at that time consisted of one lonely Swedish girl, not a bit clean and brisk as they look on travel posters, but dim, melancholic, and I suspect suicidal: she used to weep into the washing-up. She said she wept for homesickness, but I thought it was something much more cosmic and tried to talk to her about it, but she disliked me for being indirectly her employer and would simply scowl when I approached her. She couldn't deal with breakfast for all of us, poor girl, and was always half-asleep and yawning as she swayed in with the eggs and coffee. Once Papa called her a slut – not to her face, of course, but he said it – and Mama immediately launched into tirades of abstract liberal fervour while I burst into tears, totally unexpectedly, and I never knew whether it was because I hated to hear my father be so brutal or my mother so rhetorical, or whether (as I hope it was) I cried because I felt so sorry for her, depressed amongst the alien dishes. I kept telling myself that she could leave if she wanted, but it did not comfort me, for where is a gloomy young foreigner to go? I had been *au pair* myself and knew what it could feel like. She wore long black jerseys with loose sleeves rolled back, and had prominent (not protruding, prominent) white eyes, rather like a large bird – a goose or a seagull – staring and blind. She was not ideal company at the breakfast table: she seemed to echo Louise's own un-made-up pallor. The toast was hard, there was an egg short so I had to go without, and Daphne's hair had clearly been in over-effective rollers. I felt too dreary to express until I discovered amongst Louise's plentiful post a card from Martin.

It said, platitudinously enough: 'Dearest Sarah, I hope you had a good crossing and enjoy the wedding. I miss you here. Please write soon. Much love, Martin.'

Not much in the way of passion, perhaps, but these uninspired words lifted me out of my gloom and restored my faith in life: I felt a great pang for Martin and *vin ordinaire* which managed to put Louise and hard toast in their place again. It detached me, that unimpressive little postcard, and my detachment lasted until I had actually zipped myself into my bridesmaid's dress half an hour before we were due to leave for church.

I began to get involved again when I went to see if I could help Louise dress. This was one of the tasks which books on weddings expressly allocate to the chief bridesmaid, which I assumed I was, though nobody had ever said anything about it; and I have always been conscientious. Our school motto was *Qui fidelis est in parvo, in multo quoque est fidelis*. I didn't knock on her bedroom door when I went in, and surprised her standing quite still and looking at herself in the mirror. Her dress was on, but open all the way down the front.

'Can I help?' I asked.

'Yes,' she said. 'You can do my dress up down the front.'

She seemed to like my doing it for her, but I didn't like the physical closeness. I wasn't used to her. She was never a one for touching people, for kissing or fighting or sitting on knees. There were a lot of little buttons, all the way from the demure high neck to the waist, and I fumbled over them. They didn't have proper buttonholes but horrid little fabric loops. I could feel her hard breasts rising and falling under my clumsy hands in her far from new brassière. I thought how like her, to wear a bra that is actually dirty on her wedding day. She must have been wearing it for the past week.

'Is this your something old?' I asked, indicating it.

'My bra? Yes, I suppose it is. I hadn't thought.'

She was millions of miles away again, all the intimacy of the night before forgotten, but perhaps that wasn't surprising. She looked vacant and worried. She started to mess around with her hair and got me to spray lacquer on the back, which I did so liberally that I could see it shining like dewdrops during the ceremony. She has coarse hair, thick and heavy and easy to manage. I thought she was thinking purely narcissistic thoughts, when she quite suddenly said, 'I say, Sarah, what do you think it would feel like to be a virgin bride?'

'Terrifying, I should think,' I said. It was something I had often considered. 'All that filthy white.'

'What do you mean?' she asked, as she started to dab scent behind her ears.

'Oh, I don't know. Surely one would feel like a lamb led to the slaughter and all that? With a bow round one's neck?'

'Yes, I suppose so. But it must be rather exciting.'

'Hardly fair on the bridegroom.'

'Do you think one would be disappointed?'

'I've no idea,' I said, as rudely as I could. I didn't want to talk female intimacies. Not with her.

'I suppose one would,' she said. 'Still, it seems a pity.'

'Why, do you mean you're missing an extra *frisson* or something?'

She looked at me sharply, through the mirror. and said, 'Oh no. I have plenty of *frissons* of my own. Plenty.'

I still remember the way she said that. It was oddly spontaneous, oddly revealing. She must have said more than she meant, or said too much what she did mean, because she immediately snapped shut again, and started to put on her veil, humming horribly through her teeth. 'Be an angel,' she said, 'be an angel and go and look at my bouquet. Bring it up to me so I can see what it looks like.'

I went, glad to get out, and pondering to myself the likely nature of those *frissons*. I wonder if anyone ever married a man they didn't like just in order to see what it felt like? Louise's bouquet was made of lilies, huge virginal lilies, very formal, with no Constance Spryery about them: they would have done equally well for an altarpiece. They were lying on the hall table: I thought, what a nerve, really, to choose flowers like that. There was something theatrical about them, as well as something ceremonious, and I wondered who the audience was. I picked up the flowers and looked at myself with them in the hall mirror and thought that I wouldn't make nearly as good a bride as Louise. I stiffened my neck and tried to look dignified, but I couldn't make it. I lacked grandeur; I looked too pink and fleshy for the white intactness of those flowers. I looked less intact than Louise, ironically enough. I looked horrifyingly pregnable, somehow, at that moment: I looked at myself in fascination, thinking how unfair it was, to be born with so little defence, like a soft snail without a shell. Men are all right, they are defined and enclosed, but we in order to live must be open and raw to all comers. What happens otherwise is worse than what happens normally, the embroidery and the children and the sagging mind. I felt doomed to defeat. I felt all women were doomed. Louise thought she wasn't but she was. It would get her in the end, some version of it, simply because she was born to defend and depend instead of to attack. I can get very bitter about this subject with very little encouragement: fortunately Michael came along and distracted me.

'Hello,' he said. 'You look gorgeous.'

'Do I really?' I said, perking up at once. After all, to be really logical I could always have shaved off my eyebrows. And since I didn't –

'Do you like my dress?' I said.

'It's lovely. Is it the same as Daphne's wearing? It can't be.'

'Oh yes it is.'

'You look knockout, SallyO.'

'Not as knockout as Louise.'

'Don't be silly, you're much prettier than Louise.'

'Oh *Michael* –'

'Are those her flowers? Christ, what an armful.'

'Terrible, isn't it?'

'Don't you get a bouquet?'

'Oh yes! Yellow roses for me.' I picked them up.

'They look fabulous. What will you have when you get married?'

'I'm not getting married. Catch me at the kitchen sink.'

'Silly.' He kissed my hand, gallantly. He's the only member of our family who ever touches anyone without wincing. I remembered how I had hated buttoning up Louise.

'You look pretty smart yourself,' I said. 'Who's in the drawing-room?'

'Oh, everyone. Except your mother. Your father's reading the paper, Mum is knitting, Daphne's looking sick and I'm drinking gin.'

'Before church?'

'Come and have one yourself.'

'No thank you. I'm waiting till the reception.'

'I say, Sally, who drank the whisky?'

'What whisky?'

'I'm sure you know what whisky. Don't you?'

'I've no idea what you're talking about.'

'There's half a bottle gone from the corner cupboard in the music-room. Your father seems to think it must be Kristin, but I thought it was probably you two. Wasn't it?'

'It certainly was not,' I said, annoyed by his knowing smile. I prefer almost anyone to be familiar with me than my family. 'If you think it was Louise you should ask her yourself.'

'Oh, I wouldn't dare. I wouldn't be so personal. But I do think someone ought to tell Uncle that it wasn't Kristin.'

'Honestly,' I said, diverting my annoyance, 'I can't imagine where Papa thinks Kristin comes from. He talks about her as though she were a kitchen-maid, but her father's a wealthy barrister in Stockholm or something. It's ridiculous. What would she do with whisky? Papa must think she's a real hard drinker if he thinks she had all that.'

'If she's the daughter of a wealthy whatnot, what's stopping her packing up and going?'

'Oh, I don't know.' I couldn't go into the twisted motives of middle-class girls with no sense of vocation, although I felt I was becoming an expert on the subject.

'Your father's a bit of a reactionary, isn't he,' said Michael, largely to prove to me that he knew what the word meant.

'About women and servants. And poor Kristin happens to be both.'

'Oh, she's all right. She's just sex-starved. That's all.'

'Oh don't be stupid,' I said, slipping back at once into my annoyed feminist we-are-frail-as-our-complexions-are mood. 'Honestly, Michael, you are stupid sometimes.' And I marched off with Louise's lilies, but I knew quite well that he was probably right, with all his odious masculine unperplexity. I would so like people to be free, and bound together not by need but by love. But it isn't so, it can't be so.

We got off to church in the end. I was highly embarrassed by having to sit next to Daphne, who looked such a total fright in her ultra-smart dress. It was a tarty dress, but at the same time it did suit me: it had a very short skirt, and I have nice legs, whereas Daphne's are muscular and shapeless round the ankles and covered in hairs and bluish pimples. Oh, the agony. If I had had any courage I would have told her to put on suntan stockings, but somehow I couldn't interfere with the awfulness of nature. It must be so frightful to have to put things on in order to look better, instead of to strip things off. She sat there, solid and yet scraggy, and she looked blind and sentimental because she had taken her glasses off. She probably was feeling sentimental, which was a waste, about Louise. I wondered what she would think if she knew how sinister, in her terms, this marriage really was. It would have taken only that little chat about virgin brides to make her start declaring just causes and impediments. I could see her, standing nobly up and interrupting the ceremony to say that to her certain knowledge her cousin Louise Bennett had, on the twenty-second of July, nineteen-fifty-eight, with Sebastian William Howell, etc, etc. And yet here she was, happening to be ignorant, going along with her yellow roses. How can people be so totally unaware of facts? It seems to me to be almost a vice, such ignorance.

When we arrived at the church there was a crowd of villagers standing round the nineteen-thirty lych-gate staring, and I wondered if she realized that they were probably saying things like: 'A pity she isn't as good-looking as the rest of the family' or 'You always get one plain bridesmaid, don't you?' I don't know if Daphne cares about her looks at all: I fear she probably does, because her clothes, though hideous, are always elaborate, not careless, and she overcurls her hair and wears a very bright red lipstick which makes her skin look pale and dead. She wears it in an effort to appear gay. How unjust life is, to make physical charm so immediately apparent or absent, when one can get away with vices untold for ever. I know one girl who, like Daphne, is a plain girl from a handsome family, featureless and thickly-made, but she is such a girl that one forgets what she looks like in the charm of her conversation. I'm glad I know someone like that or I wouldn't believe it possible. Appearances can make one such a snob. But this girl was above appearances, whilst Daphne scrabbles after them. Daphne inflicts such pain on me. She makes me confess how much I am a bitch. And Daphne, who was chased by a god and was turned into a tree to preserve her virginity. Perhaps there is some truth in that fable. Something our Daphne had preserved. Who would rape a tree?

As we waited for Louise I remembered how she once told a whole railway compartment as we went through Chesterfield station that the tower leaned over because it saw a virgin bride. I was only eleven at the time and I was deeply shocked.

When the car drew up with Louise and my father in it, one could not help but be moved. She looked so perfect. She was a photographer's dream: they could scarcely let her go in to be married, they were so entranced, and kept taking her through her dim and heavy veil. She leaned her head this way and that, obliging, serene, betraying no impatience. The spectators were thrilled;

they kept gasping in admiration. For them she was the real thing: and for me too she almost was, for that half-hour, as meaningless and pure as the flowers she carried. By virtue of form, not content. Symbol, not moral. As I finally followed her up the aisle my hands were trembling with some appropriate emotion: I could not keep the foliage round the roses still.

I calmed down after a while, after that strange primitive shock of beauty and innocence had worn off, and had a good look round, trying to spot guests I knew. I thought I saw one of my very favourite people, a would-be and probably will-be artist called Tony, but he was half-behind a pillar. The soles of Stephen's shoes looked very clean and new, side by side, as he knelt down at the altar. I had difficulty in turning over the pages of my hymn-book with gloves on, yet felt too conspicuous to start ripping them off. I got landed with all the lilies at the ring bit: they kept me very busy till the end of the service, when Loulou reclaimed them to walk down the aisle, a married woman, to a rather obscure piece of music which I fancy wasn't the Wedding March, though I'm not certain. I heaved a sigh of relief as I tripped after, thinking 'Now for the champagne.'

When we emerged into the open air the best man, who had accompanied me, said, 'Well, Christ, that's that, what a farce.'

I didn't ask him to elucidate, and I didn't find out what he had meant for months. I assumed it was just a general comment on the church and the top-hattery. The best man, in fact, terrified me even more than Stephen himself did, as he had in addition to a certain degree of fame a rather rude and handsome face and manner. He was an actor, an almost well-known one, in fact to anyone who is slightly more of a theatregoer than me he would probably qualify as being very well-known. I at first assumed that Stephen had chosen him as best man for prestige value, but afterwards discovered that they really had been close friends Apart from other reasons. They had been up at Cambridge together, and John had been in some ghastly-sounding play of Stephen's all about a truck driver, which had had a very short run at the Lyric, Hammersmith, thereby bringing both to their first public notice. He is called John Connell. I suppose success held them both together: they are just about as unlike as two people can be. Stephen is thin, prematurely ageing, and I think I have made myself clear about my opinion of his sexual qualifications, whereas John is a heavy and rather fancies himself in jeans, open-necked shirts, and coal-heaver's jackets with leather patches on the back. It's all a big game because he went to Winchester: his histrionic tendencies only bloomed at Cambridge after long repression, where I gather he was the King of the ADC. He is a megalomaniac, like most actors, but I now think that he is so through real excess of energy and not through sheer blinkered ambition. Once he said to a director who told him not to overact: 'How can you overact life?' I like that. It's much coarser than Stephen: a much thicker ideal.

I suppose all they did share was vanity: John thought himself a superman, and Stephen thought himself a super-intellect, and they ministered to each other in mutual admiration. It was odd to see them there side by side in church, so entirely different: I wish now that I had known the whole story then, I feel Louise cheated me out of an interesting *frisson* or two.

As we embarked for the reception I heard Louise say to John, 'And for God's sake have a few drinks, remember you've got to take enough for two.'

3 The Reception

I had a hard time at the reception to begin with, trying to
remember the names of business friends of my father,
and being gay with the local gentry. I felt it my duty to
deal with them before I had more than two glasses of
champagne, so I concentrated on eating stuffed prunes,
prawns, smoked salmon and suchlike. I met the Halifax
parents, who confirmed Louise's assertion that it wasn't
a pseudonym: they were very upper, but not a bit like an
ancient family. I didn't think they could be an ancient
family. I had to keep finding plausible reasons to explain
why there wasn't a display of wedding presents. The real
reason was that Louise had refused on grounds of ostentatious vulgarity – with reason, I think – but I couldn't
say that to the kindly and charming inquiries of beneficent
ladies anxious to see once more the silver cream jugs they
so painfully chose. I felt sorry for the ladies. They weren't
interested in Louise, and why should they be? They just
wanted to have a look at everything. I decided that when
I got married they could.

After what seemed hours of such fraternizing I decided
to launch out on my own and see if I could find Tony.
Before I did I inadvertently got mixed up in a conversation
with Stephen, who approached me with a vacant, spindly
walk and said:

'Well, how do you like being my sister-in-law?'

I gave this meaningless question as little attention as it
deserved, and countered it with, 'Surely you're not
drinking orange juice on your wedding day?'

'You know quite well,' he said, 'that I never drink. I've told you before that I don't like it, but you don't seem to believe me. You even accused me of affectation last time.'

'Did I really?'

'Yes, you did. And I must say that I am strongly inclined to believe that it is as much through affectation that you indulge.'

'Oh, you're quite wrong,' I said. 'I love it.'

'I think a lot of nonsense is talked about drink,' he said.

'Perhaps. But that doesn't mean it isn't nice. And I mean to say, whoever heard of a novelist who didn't drink?'

'You must have a very romantic conception of the artist. Penniless and bearded in his garret, you see him?'

'More or less, I suppose I do. Anyway I believe in extremes, don't you?'

'No no, the well-observed norm, that is what art is about. The delicacy of the perception will compensate for any lack of violence.'

I think he was quoting from one of his reviews.

'Oh yes,' I said. 'Well, I just don't believe that, I'm afraid.'

'Well, you may find you are wrong,' he said, with a superior kind of look. I hate anyone to be didactic except me. I was just looking for some retort when I caught sight of Tony's wife Gill, and immediately disengaged myself from that totally profitless encounter. Stephen can't be such a fool as he seems. But he certainly has a lot of seeming to account for.

'Excuse me,' I said, 'I see an old Oxford friend I haven't seen for years, excuse me.'

Not very elegant, but I got away. It wasn't in fact literally years since I had seen Gill: it was more like nine months. She had been up the year before me, and so had been down for over a year now. She and Tony had got married the minute she left the Porter's Lodge, more or

36

less, at the end of her last term, and had since then been living in a flat on the King's Road. I liked them both more than almost anyone; Gill and I had been almost intimate. Not quite – the gap of one year does make some difference even at university level. Also she is basically very unlike me, much more generous and obvious and unselfconscious. With no twists, or so I thought at Louise's wedding. Tony had plenty of twists, but of the sort that to me seemed like the straight and narrow.

She was talking to some Chelsea-type lady of Louise's own past, and when she saw me she broke off what she was saying at once and said, 'Sarah, how *super* to see you.'

'How super to see *you*,' I said, inanely and happily: we stood gaping and grinning at each other, trying to think of some way to get going together again. Not painfully trying, but trying. She looked much tidier than she ever used to, I noticed: she used to be a great one for home-made dresses made of hessian and painted by herself in large bold flowers, but now she was wearing a neat grey outfit that I guessed was a Young Jaeger number. Her hair was up, too, very carefully up, in a nice yellow dome.

It was she who first thought of anything to say. All this avoiding of the weather has its points, with certain people at least.

'I was thinking,' she said, 'of that wedding we watched in that church in Milan, where we went to look at the frescoes. What was it called?'

'I can't remember,' I said. 'The *Guide Bleu* stopped at Florence. San Bartolomeo, was it, or San Ambrosio? Some polysyllabic saint.'

'Wasn't it nice? And wasn't she charming? And weren't we relieved that she was charming?'

'It was so nice of her to smile at us on the way out.'

'Brides should always be beautiful, if they insist on getting married like this. For the sake of the guests. I must say that old Louise is certainly doing her stuff.'

'Yes, she is isn't she?'

'She looks wonderful.'

'That's all very well,' I said, 'but I don't think it's very dignified, really, all this to-do. I mean to say, not for someone like her.'

'Oh, if you go by appearances ... '

'I'd much rather get married in a registry office. Wouldn't you? Or rather didn't you?'

'Yes, we did,' said Gill, curtly. 'Yes, of course we did.'

Not being stupid, I quickly noticed that something was amiss, and said, 'Why, what's the matter, is something the matter with Tony? He's here all right, isn't he?'

'Oh, yes, he's somewhere around here,' she said. 'I think I've noticed him around somewhere.'

'What do you mean?'

'Oh, didn't you know?' she said, coldly but appealingly. 'Didn't you know that Tony and I had separated?'

I hadn't known, obviously, and was completely taken aback: they were the last couple in the world about whom I would have sensed any unease or catastrophe. They were everything that Stephen and Louise weren't, spontaneous, happy, comprehensible and so forth. I was appalled.

'How awful,' I said, glad that at least I knew her well enough to ask her what had happened instead of retreating in confusion from my *faux pas*. 'How entirely awful, what on earth happened? I thought you were both so wonderful ... '

'That's what we thought too,' she said, with an odd little smile, that turned into a grimace: she has a coarse-featured face, very mobile and gay, and all her expressions give away everything. 'Oh yes, that's what we thought too. But I don't think we think so any longer.'

'What happened? When did it happen?'

'Oh, months ago! Months ago. I can't believe you don't

know about it. I thought everyone knew. I was amazed when your mother sent the invitation to both of us together.'

'Oh, she wouldn't know anything. I suppose I didn't hear because of working for exams, and then I went to Paris at the end of term.'

'Oh yes, I heard you were in Paris. I had a letter from Simone, she said she'd met you on the Gare du Nord. And congratulations on your degree, we were terribly impressed . . . '

'Oh nonsense. Don't be silly. Haven't you seen Louise recently in town? I'd have thought she might have told me about you.'

'I haven't seen her for months. Certainly not since I left Tony. She mixes with frightfully smart people now, you know. What was Paris like, Sarah?'

'Oh, it was fun really. Pointless. But fun. Don't let's talk about Paris, tell me about you.'

'Oh, I don't know what to say about it really . . . I don't know how it happened. It was so odd . . . we seemed to be getting on fine at first, just a sort of prolonged Oxford but with London instead – and then we started to quarrel. It sounds so silly. We used to quarrel a lot before, but nothing like this. It's so sordid, quarrelling. We used to quarrel about such stupid things like money and food . . . and then he was painting all the time and he seemed to think that I ought to be happy just sitting around in the nude and letting him paint me, and cooking him the odd meal. And it got so bloody cold, posing, especially when they cut the electricity off and the fire wouldn't work. Oh it was awful. I wanted to do things too, I didn't like just waiting on him. I kept saying, "You could pay someone to do that." Which wasn't in fact true of course because he hadn't any money, but then I thought facts counted less than principles and it was the principle of the thing . . . It was ghastly. It got worse and worse. Once he said to me, "Put the kettle on," and I said, "Put it on yourself, I'm reading"; and he said, "Put it on, what the hell do you think you're here for?" Isn't it unbelievable? That Tony should be like that? Tony of all people? I thought he hadn't a preconception in the world. Isn't it unbelievable?'

I nodded. It was. He was the last man I could picture saying a thing like that to anyone. Stephen Halifax, yes, my father yes, even cousin Michael in a bad temper, but not Tony.

'You don't know,' she said, 'what a difference it makes not to have meals provided. To know that if you don't start peeling potatoes there won't be any potatoes. You haven't been out long enough to know.'

'No, I haven't.'

'It's too dismal. I kept saying things like that I'd be quite happy to cook if we could afford nice things, wine and pheasants and herbs and so forth, but that nobody could be happy with bread and potatoes and spaghetti – that was a lie too, though again it was true in principle – but five shillings a day, it was a bit much. I began to feel so humiliated and degraded, I can't tell you. He simply didn't see that painting and being painted aren't equally amusing . . . Anyway one day I said my parents were right, and that I'd got what I deserved, marrying a bloody foundling.'

'You didn't.'

'Oh yes I did. I knew you wouldn't believe it, we both behaved so incredibly. It was such a bloody thing to say to anyone. And the stupid thing is that I've never had the slightest feeling about his not knowing who his parents are, I mean to say it never even crossed my mind from one month to the next. It didn't seem to matter about him at all, not nearly so much as him being a painter, or having a hairy chest, or that sort of thing – but of course as soon as I said it he immediately thought I'd been harbouring a deep-seated grievance about it, some repulsion in the blood or something – and I couldn't convince him that I didn't care at all. I said to him, "I didn't say it because I meant it but because I knew it was the only thing that would really hurt you and I had to hurt you somehow." But he didn't believe me.'

'Poor Gill. Was that the end of it then?'

'Not quite. We mouldered on till the end of March, when I discovered the crowning insult, which was that I was pregnant. Think of that. I'd never thought it would happen to me, though why I thought it was so unlikely and impossible I can't imagine. I felt ruined. I cried for days and days, and in the end I told him and said I'd have to get rid of it.'

'Oh *no*,' I said. I wasn't really shocked, but I was shocked by her saying it there, when wedding guests might have overheard. But she seemed oblivious. She wouldn't have cared if they had listened.

'Well, what could I do? He was terribly upset and rather nice about it really, and lent me the money, and asked if I was sure that that was what I wanted. I said yes. I really thought it was. It seems so stupid because I'm one of the only people I know who really wanted children. But I didn't want them like that. Sort of accidentally and without my consent. Poor kid, I hated it so violently, it almost stopped me hating Tony – I felt it was a leech sucking my blood. Is that abnormal? I suppose it's not, really. I did want a baby so, but I wanted it to be all proper and intentional with pink nurseries and flowers in hospital, you know. Not tied up in bits of old nightgown and smelling of turpentine.'

'It wouldn't have minded,' I said, with questionable tact and questionable truth.

'Oh yes it would. It's all very well living one's own sordid way, you can't expect babies to understand. So I got rid of it, and when I came home that afternoon I said

to Tony, "Well, that's that, and now I'm moving out."
To tell you the truth I'd hoped he'd throw his arms round
me and plead with me to stay, but he didn't, he just patted
me on the shoulder and said, "Well, if that's what you
want." He sent me to bed, and he brought me some
Ovaltine. That was nice of him, I suppose.' Her voice
trailed off, unintentionally pathetic. She meant that it
was nice of him. She really did expect so little.

'But, Gill,' I said, 'how could he throw his arms round
you when he must have thought you hated him so? He
wouldn't have known you wanted him to.'

'Perhaps he didn't. I never can realize that he doesn't
know how much I love him. I always feel so at a disadvantage, loving him so much. But I suppose that time
I'd shaken him. Perhaps he thought I didn't love him
any more.'

'Where did you go after that?'

'Oh, I went and stayed with Peter and Jessica for a bit,
and then I was rather ill so I went home, and when I was
better I moved back to London. I'm living there in Highgate now at the Studio with James and Rose and Jeremy
and all that crowd.'

'Are they all still painting?'

'Oh yes.' She smiled. 'God, they're terrible. So'm I,
but at least I know it. They really think they're serious
artists. It's so funny. I keep dabbling, but I know it's
only for me. Still, it's nice to try. Tony made me feel so
useless. Once I said to him, "I feel like a still life, I want
to *do* something", and he gave me a bit of canvas and a
few paints and said, "You paint me then." It was awful,
I was so offended, it was just the same as when my mother
used to give me a handkerchief to iron with my toy iron
on washday, so I could be grown-up like her. And the
truth is that my stuff *is* like child's painting when you
compare it with his. You know what I mean? It used not
to matter but it does now. Everything matters so much.'

'How did your mother take it?'

'Oh, with Christian forgiveness. You know.'

I did know. I knew Gill's family life almost as well as I knew my own, by a mixture of association and intuition: her parents, like mine, were middle-class, respectable, apparently cultured – her mother in fact *was* cultured, she was a very nice woman, a prison-visiting Quaker, one of those who actually do what they talk about doing. Gill had done her a grave injustice in her suggestion that she had objected to the marriage on the grounds that Tony had once been in an orphanage, since this was the one feature in Tony's history and personality that had really appealed to her. She had said to me once, in a curious *tête-à-tête* at a college sherry party – Mrs Webster was an Old Girl of our college – that she didn't object to Tony's being Nobody, in such a startlingly literal way, nor to his being a painter, but that she did object to his total lack of responsibility and social conscience, and his habitual promiscuity. How she got to hear of the latter I can't imagine, nor can I imagine how we ever got round to talking about it, as I am sure no definite words came up during our conversation: but we both knew that that was what we were discussing. I had defended Tony as much as I dared, though really there wasn't much defence to make, and I would have been slightly perturbed by the last allegation myself if I had been either Gill or her mother. All I could say was, helplessly, defending our generation, 'Yes, I'm sure you're right, I'm sure that from every practical point of view you're right, but I'm equally sure that he *is* reliable, on some deeper level. I'm sure he is. And it isn't security that Gill wants, not security of that sort, I know it isn't.' And now, it seemed, I had been wrong. He hadn't been reliable on any level. He was as unsound with people as he was with things and sex and money. It seemed a nasty victory to common sense, and I asked myself if it justified Louise, and then realized that Mrs Webster was as alien to Louise as she was to Tony. Why did I want to reconcile everything? Why couldn't I jump for the unreliable with both eyes shut, as Gill had done? Why did I want to have my cake and eat it, as far as security was concerned? How could one expect people to be reliable about some things and not about others? *Qui fidelis est in parvo*, I expect, though the idea nauseates me.

Depressed by this sad story, I asked Gill what she was going to do next: she seemed neither to know nor to care. I was impressed by her nonchalance. Her hair had begun to escape from its pins, shaken out of its elaborate back-combed beehive by the vehemence of her denunciation of her husband: she looked more like herself. She said, loudly, 'I expeat everyone's been listening in to this little chat, don't you think? It ought to warn people off. Talk about blighting the marriage hearse with a few odd tears.'

The phrase had crossed my mind too, but I try to resist the temptation to talk in quotations. Sometimes it seems the only accomplishment my education ever bestowed on me, the ability to think in quotations.

I wanted to get away from Gill in order to find Tony, so I deftly introduced her to Michael, who was lurking around, and slipped off with some phrase about looking for Louise. I did in fact find Louise, on the same errand: she and Tony were talking to each other in a corner. They were so engrossed that I had to tap Tony on the shoulder to interrupt: when he saw it was me his response couldn't have been more gratifying. He opened his arms and enfolded me, and I felt champagne from his glass trickling down the nape of my neck.

'*Tony*,' I said, 'you're spilling things on me.'

'Am I?' he said, as he released me and looked at me and kissed me on the cheek, making the most of everything as he always does.

44

'I should be careful,' said Louise, sourly. 'He's very tight by now.'

'Of course I am,' said Tony, 'of course I am, with all this lovely free champagne, and drinking healths to Louise, my beautiful first love. She really was, too, you know,' he said, turning to me. 'She was my first love. When I first went up, I saw Louise walking along the street in some tight cream trousers and a tight white jersey, and I said Aha, what a girl. I tracked her for days, to and fro along the road to that dismal place of yours I grew to know so well, with my heart in my mouth, wondering what she'd say if I accosted her. I didn't dare to draw near, I was quite ill with undeclared passion.'

'You great liar,' said Louise. 'I met you at Sebastian's.'

'Yes, I know I did. But that doesn't mean I hadn't followed you for weeks, does it?'

'You're a great liar. As well as everything else.'

'Oh, those were the days,' said Tony. 'Those were the days, you in those trousers, and lectures, and gowns, and bicycles, and you the most beautiful girl in Oxford. And to think you've gone and got married. It's a tragedy, that's what it is.'

'Well you did it yourself.'

'So I did. How foolish of me.'

'What should I have done otherwise?'

'Oh, don't ask me. Something grand and wicked.'

Louise smiled. She smiled and looked down at her hands, and twisted the shiny unscratched wedding ring, sitting so neatly by the great lump of diamonds. Then she said:

'I don't know, it's all rather vulgar, isn't it, getting married? I don't know what faint memory of good taste stopped me painting my nails. I was going to do them orange. Oh, but then, of course, that wouldn't have gone with my other dress . . . oh, there's always a reason for things, isn't there?'

'You couldn't look vulgar if you tried,' said Tony. 'You look like the picture of the Snow Queen in my first fairy story book. Ice within and ice without, the aristocrat of the nursery world, none of that Cinderella or Hansel and Gretel plebeian stuff, you know.'

'Oh, pack it up,' said Louise. 'I'm sick of being called heartless. I'm very tender-hearted, you know.'

'Oh yes, oh yes,' said Tony. 'That wasn't what I was calling in question. I'm sure your heart is all that it should be. And now, perhaps, you'd like to drift off and talk to your guests while your sister and I have a little chat?'

'Do you think I should?' she said, very wide-eyed and very annoyed. 'Yes, perhaps you're right, perhaps I should. I'll be seeing you some day, I suppose.'

'I suppose so,' said Tony. And she disappeared.

'Honestly,' said Tony, as she receded, 'she should go on the stage. She really should. She'd bring the house down. Tender-hearted, indeed. She probably is, to insults. All really selfish people think they're tender-hearted, because they get hurt so often. They mistake the pangs of wounded pride for the real thing.'

'Oh, she's all right,' I said, vaguely. I enjoyed hearing Tony treat her with such little respect. It reduced her. He really seemed to think that she was silly: I didn't know how he had the nerve, but I admired him for it. Well, no, I didn't exactly admire him for it, but I liked him for it. I liked him so much. I really did think he probably had treated Gill very badly. And yet, in some way, it was impossible to mind. He has that knack of suspending judgement, which is what some people mean by charm. He doesn't deceive, he simply suspends one's judgement. He is a great opportunist both with girls and with money, and yet he always gets away with it: I doubt if people ever feel wronged by him, despite the obvious incriminating facts. On the contrary, girls in particular usually seem to feel they have let him down, because what he wanted was clearly something more than mere change, and they feel guilty because he hasn't found it with them. This made the Gill affair all the more curious, because she and I, before I had seen him, had felt that he was deeply in the wrong. Perhaps there is something in the very name of marriage that had altered the case: I had had different expectations, despite my high protestations of freedom from reverence. Perhaps, in that, my sin of preconception was greater than his. Anyway, whatever the explanation of the moral undertones, the fact is that when Tony turned to me, after his comment on Louise, and said, 'Look, Sarah darling, I saw you talking to Gill and let's not us go over all that nonsense, shall we?' any annoyance that was left ebbed out of me: under the solid heaviness of his presence it seemed unreal, theoretical, a mere head-idea, and I was where I had always been, friendly and overcome with delight that such lovely people exist. Also, I must confess, at the risk of sounding a fool which I am not, that when he said darling to me the word hit me in the stomach: it isn't a word he uses casually, and he had said it with real intimacy, which is so rare a thing that it brings the tears to my stupid eyes whenever it is proffered. And so, thawed, I smiled and said, 'Well, then, what shall we talk about? Did you send Lou away so that we could talk about her?'

'Oh no! Not her. I thought we might note all the guests. All their qualities.'

'We might,' I said, 'if desperate for other topics.' I didn't mean that: I loved noting people, especially with somebody else. Tony and I had spent many a happy hour sitting on bridges and punts taking sociological surveys, and now, as I looked round with him at all the hats and bow-ties and champagne glasses, everything became suddenly full of the subaqueous glamour of existence, no longer gestures, but the things themselves.

'I'd have thought they were rather good material for noting,' he said. 'I've never seen such a fabulous mixture of varieties of money. I must be the only pauper here. Why aren't there any more people from Oxford?'

'Oh, I don't know. They're all abroad, or working, or can't afford the train fare, I suppose. Or perhaps they can't be bothered to come. Why did you come, in any case? I'd never have expected a lazy lump like you to come all this way.'

'Why shouldn't I come? I was asked.'

'Yes, I know you were.'

'Oh, I came for various reasons. Somebody was going up to Birmingham in a car, and I've got to see someone else in Stratford tomorrow. And then I wanted to see Louise at her final exit. And I wanted to see you. You're old friends of mine, aren't you?'

'Well, in a manner of speaking. But don't tell me that friendship overcomes inertia.'

'Not by itself, naturally.'

'I suppose I came all the way from Paris myself, now I come to think of it. Pretty stupid thing to do, just for Louise. When Paris was so nice.'

'Was it?'

'Oh, heaven. I can't think why I left. I met an absolutely wonderful man called Martin who worked in a bookshop, and he spoke such wonderful French that everyone thought he was, he could talk as quickly as they do and without thinking. We had a wonderful time. He knew all the odd people, you know, American painters and vagrants and so forth. Why do I always like vagrants more than inhabitants? More than sensible, solid, respectable people like Stephen?'

'Sensible, solid and respectable, did you say? That archetypal madman?'

'He's not mad. Do you know him?'

'I've met him. We have friends in common. A ghastly

chap called Wilfred Smee. And believe me he's neurotic all right.'

'Who wouldn't be with a name like that?'

'I meant Stephen.'

'Oh. Oh. No, I don't agree, I think it's you that's neurotic, not him.'

'Me?'

'Yes, you. He's in with the world, you're not.'

'What do you mean by that? If anyone's in with the world, I am. I love it. I've got both my hands round it, believe me, Sarah. I can taste what I'm drinking and see what I'm seeing. I'm fantastically well-integrated.'

'Not what I call integration.'

'Perhaps you mean social integration?'

'Perhaps I do.'

'For Christ's sake, you girls. You're just like Gill. Always worrying about who fits where. And if things don't fit, you're lost.'

'That's just what I've been saying,' I said, 'but you don't listen. I like things that don't fit. I like people like Martin and you and Simone. I like people without any social bearings.'

'Oh well, if you mean people like Simone . . . '

Simone. She's not a fair counter, not even on the subject of vagrancy. Nationless, sexless, hopelessly eclectic, hopelessly unrooted: her very name puts things out of perspective.

'Simone,' he repeated. 'When did you last see Simone?'

'On the Gare du Nord. At about five in the morning.'

'What on earth were you both doing there?'

'Oh, it was very odd and charming. I'd been up all night with Martin and a boy called Yves and an American girl called Linda, one of those nights when everyone is in love with everyone else, so nobody can go to bed because that would mean deciding who to go or not go with – I liked Linda best, honestly, I was terrified of losing her to either of those men – and so we stayed up, walking around and hobnobbing with Algerians, and we ended up in the Gare du Nord trying to get a cup of coffee. They were washing those big stone ladies on top, it was just light enough to see. The coffee was foul and tepid because the machine had only just warmed up for the morning. We were just beginning to get really gritty, dirty and disagreeable when in walked Simone. I was so amazed.'

'Where had she come from?'

'She'd been sitting on a soldier's knee all the way from Marseilles, she said. She was wearing a nineteenth-century admiral's topcoat with silver buttons that she'd got out of one of her grandmother's attics in Rome.'

'He must have been a very brave soldier. To offer her his knee.'

'Oh, people don't notice on trains. They really don't. They don't employ any discrimination about who they pinch or offer their bed to or who they buy meals for. They just don't notice.'

'Not even when someone looks like Simone?'

'Apparently not. Though she can deal with people much more quickly than me. If they start anything she just spits. With real old aristocratic vehemence. There's class for you. I'm too bourgeois, I wouldn't know how to spit. Usually I daren't even protest.'

'Poor little Sarah. She lets people lift up her skirts on the Métro because she's too well-bred to object.'

'That's just about it. But you should have seen Simone. She looked so extraordinary. She made poor Linda look like a schoolgirl. You know what, she gives me such a sense of tradition and *salons* and Henry James. And yet she doesn't belong anywhere. Or perhaps she belongs everywhere. I'd like to be irresponsible like that. To be able to go on like that for ever.'

He looked at me, sharply. I was sorry I'd said what I

had said, or at least those last two phrases of it: I know that Tony despises people who don't like being exactly what they are and in many ways I sympathize, though one does need more of a tension than he will admit. And I didn't want to be Simone, or only at times.

And I didn't want to leave him, but I felt I should, and said so. The speeches and cake-cutting were due to start before long and I had to get back to Daphne and Louise for the photographs. So we parted, but before we did so Tony asked me if I'd like to spend the following day with him in Stratford. I was delighted and said yes, without thinking of Gill at all: she had dropped out of my mind. Then, feeling pleased with myself for having fixed up this infinitesimal bit of my future, I rejoined the family side of the affair. We had lots and lots of photographs and speeches, all very witty and tedious, and we drank healths: I was feeling a little hazy by this time, and full of goodwill. After that I had an impression that the etiquette book thought I ought to help Louise to change, so I followed her when she tripped off to do so. I found her giggling to herself as she struggled with her row of little buttons: 'Oh, Sally, what a joke,' she said. 'What a ghastly joke, I've drunk pints and Stephen's been on orange juice all day long.'

She trampled the dress to pieces as she was getting out of it, and she left it all heaped on the floor. Then she dressed up again in lilac; lilac to the eyeshadow: as she was standing in her skirt and bra, just about to put on her jacket, there was a knock at the door.

'Who's that?' she said.

'John,' was the reply.

'Oh, it's you,' she said, dropping the jacket on the back of the chair. 'Come in.'

'May I?'

'Oh yes, go along, come in.'

He came in, and stood in the doorway staring at her. He

looked as if he too had had too much to drink. She stared back. 'Hello,' she said, after a moment. 'What d'you want?'

'Oh, I just wanted to know if your case was ready to put in the car.'

'Trying to get rid of me?'

'You know I am.'

'All right, all right, you can have it. The white one. You've got the others.'

'Yes. I've got them.'

He picked up the case and started to go, but she suddenly said, 'Wait, wait, I've forgotten to pack my hairbrush. Wait while I do my hair.'

And then she took every single pin out of her hair and let it all down, out of its immaculately tidy arrangement, and started to brush it. She brushed it with long sweeping movements, throwing her head back at the end of each stroke, so that she showed an appalling white expanse of neck and underchin and bosom. He watched her while she did it. When she had finished brushing it she threw me the brush to pack, and started putting it all up again. When she had put it up, she put on the jacket of her suit and smiled at him, blinking and sweet. He took the suitcase and went out without a word. I thought to myself that I had never witnessed such crude and awful vanity in my life.

They got off in the end, Stephen and Louise: they drove away through the yellowing trees at forty mph towards London and the airport and Rome.

As I went to bed that night, I wondered why social events are for me such a sea of blood, sweat and tears, from which I salvage perhaps two floating words, set afloat by a providence which will not let me drown with empty hands.

4 The Move

I spent a couple of hours in Stratford with Tony and his friend the following day. His friend was a spear-carrier. Stratford was pretty, with a smell of falling poplar leaves down by Clopton bridge. We had drinks at the Duck and I heard a lot of gossip about this and that and John Connell, and a lot of theatrical jokes about missed cues, forgotten lines, and other hilarious topics. Tony seemed gloomy and depressed, largely I think because of a gloomy painter we met who was painting backcloths for the theatre and bewailing his wasted talent. He kept saying, 'Oh, I had illusions once.' I was quite impressed by how well-known and well-anecdoted John appeared to be: even I carried an aura of vicarious theatrical O K-ness through being the sister of the woman to whose husband he was best man. If you see what I mean. John was evidently somewhat of a legend-maker, always behaving outrageously on and off stage, falling asleep when he had nothing to say and so forth. I suppose I must be jealous of people like that because I got sick of hearing about him, especially as nobody had ever seen him do any of these remarkable things, but merely knew other people who had seen him. Somebody hinted that he was having an affair with an Eurasian nightclub singer, but somebody else swore that he was constantly seen with a tall and fashionable deb. I really couldn't work up much curiosity after the first half-pint or so. And I began to get positively bored when Tony started going on about Stephen. 'The trouble with that man is that he's dead from the neck down,' he kept saying, to anyone who wanted to hear, in aggressively virile tones. I began to feel annoyed with him once more for what he had done to Gill. Also, some latent sense of loyalty to Louise made me reluctant to hear such things said in public on the day after her marriage. I wondered how far they had got. To Rome? Not yet, perhaps.

In the end I had had enough of Tony and was glad to leave. I caught a convenient bus home, and we went through the fields and past the trees: the seasons had a lovely rhythm and I had none at all. As we went I thought about Louise and Stephen and John, and my thoughts became gradually clearer, somehow harmonized by the colour of the corn and the sound of the trees brushing their branches against the upstairs windows of the bus. I remembered the first and only other time when I had ever seen them all three together. It had seemed significant even at the time, but I had thought it was significant only as itself, for what it was to me, then, in my life. It had been only a few months earlier, in May or June, while I was working for Finals at Oxford. It was a Saturday morning: I was sitting in the college library with a great pile of books and a few pieces of file-paper trying to make notes on something when Simone came in. I gave her a faded smile and looked down again but she came over to me and said, 'There's your sister and two men wandering around looking for you downstairs. I showed them to your room.'

'Who?' I said, incredulously.

'Your sister and two men.'

'How the hell did they get in?'

'I don't know.' Simone was being offhand about the situation.

'Oh damn,' I said. 'I'd just got so nicely settled down.'

'Don't go then,' said Simone.

By this time everyone was looking up from their books and staring at us, which didn't trouble her, though it troubled me, so I got up to go. I wanted to take all my books with me, as it had taken me hours to assemble them, so I had to write slips out for each one of them, under the eye of the librarian, who must have known that I had approximately three times my quota of books in my room. I was afraid Louise, never very assiduous in her pursuit of me, would have gone by the time I got there. It was a good quarter-mile of corridor to my room, and on the way I began to grow conscious of my early-morning-in-college, un-made-up, bedroom-slipper, academic look. I was even more conscious of it when I arrived, pushed open the door, and saw Louise and her two men. It was a sunny day and my room looked delightful, full of dust, flowers, books and unmade bed. Louise was sitting on the window-seat, in white trousers and a white shirt, and the two men were standing around in the fireplace region. They all started as I came in: they had obviously been talking about something. I recognized Stephen, but I had never met John before, though I knew who he was.

'Hello,' I said. 'What are you doing here?'

'Just visiting,' said Louise. She didn't move a muscle. The sun was shining through the window into the room: she looked dazzling, as though the light were shining through her too.

'Just visiting. We thought we'd call on you.'

'Thanks a lot,' I said, and put my pile of books down on the top of my desk.

'I trust that we haven't interrupted your studies?' said Stephen.

'Not half,' I said. 'I was just settling down for a quiet day in the library.'

'On a day like this?'

'It's always like this at exam time,' I said.

'You haven't met John, have you, Sarah?' said Louise, still from her distant point of sunny vantage. 'This is John Connell. John, this is my little sister Sarah.'

'How do you do,' I said.

'How do you do,' he said.

You couldn't deny that he was stunning. He seemed to fill the room, and Stephen looked more nebulous than ever by his side.

'Well,' I said, 'shall we all have a cup of coffee?'

'I thought we'd go out,' said Louise.

'Come to that,' I said, 'how did you get in?'

'Through the back door.'

'Well, I hope nobody saw you. My name will be mud.' Men weren't allowed in college during the mornings.

'Oh, nobody saw us,' said Louise, 'I know my way around here.'

They all looked so odd in my room, so much older than anyone I ever remembered having been in it before, so much older and so much smarter.

'Where are we going out to?' I asked.

'I don't know. In Stephen's car. To the country.'

'Where on earth have you all come from?'

'Oh, from London. It seemed a nice day to go out.'

'Do you really want me to come?'

'Yes, of course we do. That's why we came to pick you up.'

'Oh.' I said. 'Well, if we're going out I'll have to change my skirt.'

'All right,' said Louise, 'carry on.'

And they really seemed to be expecting me to carry on, and as I hadn't the nerve to throw them out in the corridor, apart from the risk of their being discovered there, I did so. I didn't at all mind taking off my tatty old skirt in front of John, for some reason, possibly because he was an actor and with actors such things hardly register, but I very much minded in front of Stephen. Even though I was wearing a totally opaque black petticoat. They all looked the other way as I got a reasonable skirt out of the wardrobe and put it on: there was something in Stephen's personality that made any attempt at informality a mockery, even though he himself was ostensibly a Bohemian type, at least in dress and opinion. I simply didn't know what kind of behaviour he expected from me.

As I brushed my hair and dabbed on a little lipstick, Louise got up and wandered over to my desk, and started reading my essay, the one I had been making notes for in the library. She read the title out aloud: 'In the *Leviathan*, Hobbes demonstrates nothing adequately except the limitations of his own study-bound conception of human nature.'

'Well, well, well,' she said. 'That's quite a thing to write about, isn't it? Where's the quotation from?'

'I made it up,' I said. 'I couldn't find anything I wanted to write on, so I made it up.'

'Oh,' she said, dryly, 'it gets you a long way, that kind of thing, writing essays on human nature, you know. You really find an awful lot out, studying other people's study-bound conceptions of human nature in your own study, don't you?'

'Yes, I think you do,' I said, crossly. I thought it was rather low of her to start taking it out of me for being academic, when she had been through it all herself. And especially mean at exam time. 'I think I'm going to write rather a good and original essay, if you really want to know.'

'I'm sure you are,' she said. 'I'm sure it's all very valuable.'

And I am sure I detected a note of wistfulness and nostalgia in her voice at that moment, a nostalgia that she covered up the moment after with, 'Really, Sarah, do you always leave your underclothes strewn about the room?'

'I wasn't expecting visitors,' I said, pushing a pair of pants under the bed with one foot. Not that I really minded about them. 'I haven't time for all that nonsense.'

'Come on,' said John, 'let's go.'

'All right. But if anyone sees us, don't try claiming any acquaintance with me.'

We got out unobserved, fortunately, and found Stephen's car parked outside. I must confess that it was more the thought of the car that had lured me away from my books than the prospect of Louise's company. I adore cars. And it really was a most gloriously sunny day: far too good for Hobbes and the college library.

I was hardly surprised at all to see Louise, although it was the first time she had ever visited me in Oxford since she herself went down two summers before. I knew exactly why she had come to see me. There is something about Oxford in the summer that is so entirely under-graduate and nostalgic and enclosed that a visitor feels compelled to establish some contact with the university world: it sucks people in. Uncles look up nephews they had never meant to visit, and passing girls look up long-forgotten men just for the sake of a ride in a punt or tea in a college garden. Having once arrived in Ox, Louise had inevitably come to see me, partly in order to display Stephen and John to me, and partly in order to display me to Stephen and John. For although I knew Louise wasn't an admirer of mine, I wasn't too humble to realize that to these three people from London I had the pure virtue of being the real thing, the real student with a real pile of books and a real gown and a real essay to write. It was my place, Oxford, and I was on my own ground, for the only time in the history of my acquaintance with those three.

It was nearly lunch-time and we drove out to eat some-where out of Oxford. I wanted to go out of the town, as I so rarely had the chance. I thought we would probably go to a pub, but we ended up in rather an expensive hotel just off the road to Banbury. If there is anything that fills me with as much enthusiasm as cars, it is hotels, so I was transported with quiet and concealed joy. We drank a lot of Pimm's at the bar, and then went and ate a lot of delicious food: Louise always eats an enormous amount and never puts on an ounce. So do I and neither do I. I noticed one curious thing while we were eating: Stephen never seemed to know what to order, and when his food arrived he messed about with it quite horribly, covering it with salt and pepper and French mustard and olive oil, and never more than half-finished anything. He didn't drink, either: I remember thinking how dreary it must be, to be stone cold sober when everyone else is pleasantly mellow. The talk was quite pleasant: Louise and John talked about the theatre, Stephen and I talked about books and novelists, and so on. Stephen seemed to admire all the people I admired, except for Kingsley Amis. It annoyed me, as I was sure he liked them all for the wrong reasons. He talked about them so professionally, whereas these things were life and death to me. When he said, of a novel I particularly admired, 'Of course, the whole thing would have been much more effective had he set it in a slightly lower social setting,' I almost lost my temper, as I am apt to do.

'What do you mean?' I said. 'He was writing about those people because those were the people he was writing about, and that's the end of it.'

'Oh no it isn't,' he said. 'His ideas would have come across much more clearly had he allowed himself a wider field for contrast.'

'But it isn't about ideas, it's about people,' I said, crossly.

'Not about individual people. Only about people as they illustrate a point.'

'And you think the point could have been better illustrated in another way?'

'That's it.'

'But if he'd changed the social setting he'd have changed everything. The problems as well as the ideas, wouldn't he?'

'Why would he?'

This professional obtuseness baffled me, and I gave up and went back to my strawberries and cream.

At the end of the meal they asked us if we would have coffee in the garden. It was a lovely garden, with lawns and trees and roses: we sat around dozily in the sun. After a while I began to think it was time I left, as I had to meet someone for tea, so I hinted that I ought to be going.

Louise and I went to the Ladies while Stephen or John or both paid the bill: in the Ladies, as I combed my hair, I said to Louise, 'Are you working at the moment?'

'I've given up work' said Louise. 'It doesn't get you anywhere. I have other things in hand.'

'Such as what?'

'Oh, this and that.'

'What was your last job?'

'Advertising.'

'How deadly.'

'There are worse things. What are you going to do when you come down?'

'I haven't thought.' And I hadn't, either. It didn't seem to matter at the time.

'It takes a lot of thinking,' said Louise.

After a pause, I said, 'It was a lovely meal. I love food.'

'So do I.'

'I feel wonderful,' I said, and meant it. I was extremely happy, all that term, and particularly, that day.

'You look it,' said Louise, without looking at me. I was embarrassed by her tone.

'I wish I could eat like that every day,' I said. 'Every day of my life.'

'Oh, one can't have everything,' said Louise. 'It's either lovely food or lovely company.'

'Of course one can have everything,' I said. 'Have one's cake and eat it. I intend to.'

'I daresay you do,' she said. 'So did I.' She paused, and

then said, in a different tone, a tone of intention rather than expectation, 'and so do I. So do I.'

I didn't see what she meant. Not for ages. Not until I learned myself how difficult it was to get anything, let alone the everything that is showered on one in garlands and blossoming armfuls until one faces the outside world.

So we drove back to Oxford. I was in the back of the car with John, who asked me some rather intelligent questions about Finals. Like Louise, he wasn't as dumb as he ought to have been with those looks. Why is Life so unevenly distributed? I was full of envy for those two, or would have been if I hadn't then been so perpetually full of envy for myself.

Times had certainly changed since then, I reflected, as the bus arrived at our village post-office. For her and for me. Now I was at a loose end and she was married. And moreover I didn't know any rich men with cars to pass the time away by feeding me in restaurants and driving me round the countryside. I wondered at the skill with which Louise infallibly picked up wealth. I suppose I could have done it once if I had really tried. I used to know a very rich man whose father was something to do with Barclays Bank. But then he was even more boring than Stephen. One can't have everything.

It was on that bus-ride that I realized that I really would have to get a job. Even Louise had gone into advertising. Although since that meeting in May I don't think she had worked at all.

The next day I had a letter from Gill. She said that if I was thinking of going to live in London, why didn't we look for a flat together.

The next day I broached the subject to my mother. Our discussion went along these well-oiled grooves.

ME: Mummy, I've been thinking, I think I might go to London at the end of the week.

MAMA: [Pause] Oh yes?

ME: Yes, a friend of mine wants someone to share a flat and I thought it would be a good opportunity for me to . . .

MAMA: Well, that sounds a very good idea. Where exactly is this flat?

ME: Well, we haven't exactly got one, but I thought I might go and look – it's easier if you're on the spot.

MAMA: Oh yes, I'm sure it is. I hear it's very difficult to find flats in London these days.

ME [my heart sinking as I think of adverts, agencies, *Evening Standards*, *etcetera*]: Oh no, it's not at all difficult, people get themselves fixed up in no time.

MAMA: Oh well, I suppose you know better than me. What will you live on while you're there?

ME: I'll get a job. I'll have to sometime, you know. I'll write to the appointments board.

MAMA: Just any sort of job?

ME: Whatever there is.

MAMA: Don't you want a proper *career*, Sarah? I mean to say, with a degree like yours . . .

ME: No, not really, I don't know what I want to do.

MAMA: I'm not sure I like the idea of your going off all the way to London without a proper job and with nowhere to live . . . still, it's your own life, I suppose. That's what I say. No one can accuse me of trying to keep you at home, either of you . . . Who is this friend of yours?

ME: A girl called Gill Slater. She was at Oxford. She was here at the wedding, she knows Louise.

MAMA: Oh yes, the girl in grey with all the long hair . . . I thought she was married?

ME: Married? Oh no.

MAMA: I'm sure I addressed the invitation to a Mr and Mrs Antony Slater.

ME: Oh *Antony*. That's her brother. Perhaps Louise put

them on the list as Antony and Gill Slater, did she?

MAMA: Yes, that must have been it. How silly of me. They must have been surprised. And they did reply separately, I remember now – oh well, it's too late to worry. And what does she do?

ME: Oh, she's a – she's a sort of research student.

MAMA: Oh yes? Well, it sounds like a very nice idea. After all, you won't want to stay here all your life cooped up with your poor old mother, will you? I shall lose all my little ones at one fell swoop, shall I?

ME: Oh don't be silly.

MAMA: What do you mean, don't be silly? It seems to me you're very eager to be off.

ME: You know that's not it at all.

MAMA: Well, what is it then?

ME: Well, it's just that I can't stay here all my life, can I?

MAMA: No, of course you can't, nobody ever suggested anything of the sort. When have I ever tried to keep you at home? Haven't I just said that you must lead your own life? After all, that's why we sent you off to Oxford, it was always me who said you two must go – I don't know what I wouldn't have given for the opportunities you've been given. And your father wasn't any too keen, believe me. In my day education was kept for the boys, you know.

ME: Well, you hadn't any boys to educate, had you? You had to make do with us.

MAMA: And what thanks do I get? And you can't say that staying at home for a week just after you've got back from abroad is staying at home *all your life*, can you? I've hardly had a chance to see you yet, and you're off. I sometimes wonder what you and Louise bother to come home for . . . Oh, it's all very well when you want something, like a bed or a reception, but as for staying here for me, it never crosses your minds, does it?

ME: Honestly, Mama, you know you always used to get

furious when Louise came home . . . and I have to start earning my living sometime, don't I?

MAMA: I don't see what all the hurry is about. No sooner do I get rid of one daughter than the other starts leaving home. You just use home as if it were a hotel, you two, you don't seem to remember I'm your mother and have always been on your side whenever your – and then all you want to do is to get away to your horrible dirty friends and horrible poky little flats.

ME: Oh, Mum, you know Loulou's flat isn't a bit horrible, it's a very smart little place in South Ken, all pastel painted and hand-woven curtains . . .

MAMA: All I am is a servant, that's all I am, just a household drudge, and when I think how I respected my mother and carried things for her, and the years I've sat in for you two, all those nights when your father was away . . .

ME: Don't say that, don't say that, of course I'll stay, it doesn't matter to me at all . . .

MAMA [in floods of tears]: Oh, I know there's nothing to keep you here, I know there's no reason why you should stay here, there's nothing to amuse you, you've outgrown it all, you always were too clever for me . . .

ME [weeping too, feeling myself saying her words, wounded by my own sharp, indifferent self]: Oh don't, please don't, Mummy, please don't, I'll stay with you as long as you like, you know I will . . .

MAMA [sniffing and reasserting her hairpins]: No, don't be silly. Of course you can't stay here, what on earth would you do with yourself here? You go off to London, you'll be better off there, it's your duty to get yourself a good job . . .

ME: No, I don't want to go any more.

MAMA: Oh yes, you really ought to go. It would be much better for you to go. So let's have no more nonsense, shall we?

And so I went to London at the end of the week. Once a point has been made openly my mother never retracts: she has a high sense of honour, at least theoretically, and occasionally I feel obliged to hold her to the letter of what she has said and not the spirit of it. This was one of those cases. I stayed at first in a flat at Earl's Court with an old school-friend, a strange relic from my subdued past: at school we used to get out of bed at midnight and go down to sit in the moonlit classroom amongst the empty desks, where we would talk about John Donne, Camus and Comus. Now she was training to be a probation officer: the moral streak had come out on top, and although she still regarded it with a certain detached suspicion, I could see that she had settled down to live with it in close communion. I admired her perseverance: I envied her her acquaintance with Teds and shop girls: but I felt little impulse to go and do likewise. And I didn't feel it was wholly my own love of luxury that was preventing me, either: I felt it was something slightly more positive. My moral streak was more ravenous and more demanding: I couldn't satisfy it with a sacrifice.

In the end I got a job with the BBC. It seemed better than nothing, and it was work, with all the added charms of coffee-breaks, desks, lifts and catching the Tube home. Though I hadn't as yet got a home. For some reason I didn't get in touch with Tony, in his loathsome flat in the King's Road, but I did ring Gill. She asked me out to visit her in the place in Highgate where she was living, and when I got there I saw at once why she was keen to get out. It was unspeakably sordid, and like Tony's place it stank of paint: all the people in it were trying to be artists, though they completely lacked talent, and made Tony look like a young Picasso. They were all very young, younger even than Gill and me, and they all wore large men's jerseys of shattering expense, and smoked all the time. I suppose such a place could have had charm if I had met it at the right moment: it could even have had glamour if I had gone there straight from leaving school: but as I was preoccupied with flats and jobs and being serious it utterly repelled me. I kept remembering my mother's comments about dirt. It wasn't just that they kept the bread loose on the windowsill among the ashtrays, without a suggestion of a breadboard, and cooked in unwashed pans, and left stale Martini in the only teapot: I could have thought these habits endearing, if it hadn't been for the phoneyness of the whole setup. And these were such phoneys that I couldn't even pride myself on detecting them. I felt as though I were watching them all through the civil pages of one of Stephen's short stories about Bohemia. I hated the way they all felt it their duty to be rude, frank and blunt. I felt in relation to them as my probation officer friend doubtless felt in relation to me. Squalor has its degrees, like crime.

Gill and I didn't have too bad a time flat-hunting. We kept drawing little circles on the map, indicating areas that we couldn't bear to live outside, and in the end found somewhere in our third and largest circle, through an ad in a window, moreover, not through an agency. It was in Highbury, at the top of Highbury Hill, in a large decayed Victorian house. It was on the second floor, and the rooms were vast and gracious, with ceilings covered in moulded fruit and flowers. Gill borrowed a ladder from a neighbourly carpenter and painted all the moulding red and green and gold. It looked quite homely. The best thing was that we had enough room: I couldn't have shared a bedroom, I don't think. We settled down together there in a kind of suspended, interim tranquillity: Gill was working, quite pointlessly, at Swan & Edgar's, and I was busy filing things at the BBC. The days passed, which seemed the most I could expect of them, and the weather gathered its cold strength for the attack of winter.

After a while I began to wonder what had happened to

Louise. Nobody had heard anything of her: she hadn't even sent my parents a postcard to say she'd arrived in Rome. But I knew that she couldn't have come home, as the news would surely have filtered through to me had she been in London. One October evening as I was walking home from the bus stop I passed a film poster of some epic with a large picture of the Coliseum, and I suddenly and insistently remembered her. I wondered why she was such a mystery, why she didn't fit together, why she was so unpredictable. I simply could not imaginer what she and Stephen were doing together in Rome, if indeed they were still there: I could never picture one of their conversations together when nobody else was there. They just didn't exist in relation to each other. And yet I suppose that I knew more facts about Louise than anyone else in the world, except perhaps our mother: but despite this I had a much better sense of what Gill, for example, would do under any given circumstances. I felt my powers of deduction were at fault: I ought to have been able to deduce from observed particulars, whereas I always trust to messy things like intuition, or to sheer voluntary information and confessions. I was just telling myself that it was time I had a little more data about Louise's case when I arrived at our front door. I put my hand in the letter-box, and there, like a polite reply to my half-formulated thinkings, lay a letter from Simone, with a Rome postmark.

I went upstairs with it in a glow of contentment, feeling it solid and thick in my hand, a large white and expensive envelope covered in Simone's black, twig-like script. A whole letter, and it felt quite a long one. It was so long since she had written to me: her letters used to arrive during vacations like manna in the wilderness. And I realized by my gratitude how near to a wilderness was the place I was now inhabiting. I made myself wait to open it until I had taken off my coat, hung it on the peg, lit the gas fire and sat down on the hearthrug: then I ran my finger through the thick, stiff paper and took out the neatly folded sheet. Her writing looked like some other language, hieroglyphic, neat and unearthly. Not for her the unaesthetic carelessness of dashes, scribbles, and postscripts.

Roma

Sara cara cara mia,

How enchantingly your name suits this enchanting language, and how repentant I am for my long silence since I saw you in the summer at that station. I would write, but then what would I say? I have death in my heart.

To resume. I was reminded of you by meeting your sister Louise, whom I last saw three years ago in Oxford, *blasé* and breathless after three years of conquest: at first sight she reminded me of that piece which begins 'They that have power to hurt and will do none.' I met her this time not on a station but in a church, that other refuge of the aimless. In Santa Maria in Cosmedin. Do you remember it? All those layers of all those centuries, Rome, Byzantium, and the dark ages of the world, and I might harden into less than one grain of one pillar. Also those barley sugar things around the altar are very consoling, so frivolous in all the serious stonework. And there I met your sister Louise, half-heartedly inspecting the half-vanished frescoes, and alone on her honeymoon. She was looking more beautiful than in Oxford: in Oxford she had the air of an heiress up for the weekend, coldly distinct in the midst of all those pre-Raphaelite daisy-nibbling barefoot Beatrices who swept the city in our era. But in Rome she looked herself, posed expensively against an artistic background. She was all in black and white and grey, and there was something stoic and stony in her face that suited the masonry. I thought I would avoid her, but she saw me and spoke to me, so we went and sat outside by the yellow fountain, where she told me she had married Stephen Halifax (and I hate *cara mia* his insufferable books) and that he was lunching with a film director. I would like to have that Vestal Virgin's House at the bottom of my garden.

As she talked inattentively of this and that I thought of those lines of Joachim du Bellay, which he once wrote of Rome:

'Si le temps peut finir chose si dure
Peut finir la peine que j'endure.'

My pain I know is without end: I am after all nothing more than a neo-Gothic ruin, built in decay for the bats and the ivy: but hers, hers I cannot help comparing with your more curable afflictions, and I wonder if those enchanting eyes will ever gaze at anything other than the imagined glass?

You will forgive me, Sara de mon coeur, for writing to you of your sister: it is an oblique overture to you, one of the more happy incidents in that succession of journeys and train tickets which is my life.

Mon âme s'envole vers toi.

Simone

I finished her letter and then looked down at it with a glow of pleasure: Simone's letters are always a delight, they always reassure and assert something in me which is usually crying out for satisfaction. I am so relieved and excited that she continues to remember me: I see her as so much greater and grander than myself, that her recognition is like a bow from a queen. And she clearly remembered that meeting on the Gare du Nord as tenderly as I did: she would say to our acquaintances all over Europe, 'I met Sarah, you know, at five in the morning . . . ' My life was thereby extended into bars and trains and drawing-rooms that I would never enter. I was distinguished by her attention from people like Daphne, who was never an incident for anyone. I was *cara Sara*, and I am a fool about endearments. I wonder, is there something servile in my admiration for Simone? Because I do admire as well as love her, though I have always believed love preferable to an exclusive of admiration. I consider her a superior being. She is superior, and in contact with her I share her superiority: I lose the cruel and evasive sentimentality that Daphne and my mother arouse in me, and I become created harder and brighter in her eyes.

Her writing is so beautiful. So spiked and classy on the page. The first time I saw it was when she called on me in college after meeting me at a party: I was out, and she left me a note on white, thick-grained paper with a flower stuck through the sheet, a black twig with one yellow flower like a Japanese painting, and never since then have I seen her writing without the image of that twig and that leafless, austere yellow flower. It was so like her, so deliberately chosen: or perhaps people choose their own symbols naturally, for Gill always has in her room vast masses of green leaves, any leaves, chopped off trees or hedges, whilst Stephen and Louise have dried grasses in long Swedish vases. Simone, the flower without the foliage, and Gill, the foliage without the flower. I should like to bear leaves and flowers and fruit, I should like the whole world, I should like, I should like, oh I should indeed.

Sad, eclectic, gaunt Simone with her dark face and her muddled heritage, her sexless passions and her ancient clothes, gathered from all the attics of Europe. She is the window through which I first glimpsed the past. Her mother was a French opera singer and her father an Italian general: their houses, she once told me, were full of dead laurel wreaths and medals and pictures of the dead. She herself moves through a strange impermanent world where objects are invested with as much power as people, and places possibly with more: these things have for her a pure aesthetic value, totally divorced from the world of sensations and rhythms where I live. Tragic Simone, cut after an unlivable pattern. She is the most singular character in the subversive feminine realm which men are so ready to resent and to misunderstand: even Tony, who is sympathetic to most of the loose vagaries of the passions, would have called my feelings towards her nothing but decadent emotionalism. I can just hear him saying those very words – words which he would never have used about any man, no matter how decayed. Friendships between women are invariably described pejoratively as intimacies, sublimations or perversions, but I don't believe that Simone offered or experienced any of these things. Men and women were the same to her, unsmeared by any image of profit or loss or by the over-hanging future: she had no future. She was most purely personal in her life. In most people, and in myself, I am vaguely aware of a hinterland of non-personal action, where the pulls of sex and blood and society seem to drag me into unwilled motion, where the race takes over and the individual either loses himself in joy or is left helplessly self-regarding and appalled. With her I sensed a wholly willed, a wholly undetermined life. And how could such a person live? The French believe they can, but one has only to read their books to mark some heroic dislocation from the pulse of continuous life. She lacked an instinct for kitchens and gas-meters and draughts under the door and tiresome quarrels: and, lacking instinct, she had to live on will. Willing to get up, willing to go to bed, willing to eat or sleep or love.

And where does one get the energy for this sort of existence? The only way to be recharged is to be put in touch with external rhythms. Otherwise one will run down from exhaustion. Simone will run down, in a train or a gutter or a hotel bedroom, like those *fin-de-siècle* poets she so much admires and resembles. I know it, I know the signs of a short term, though she is the only living person in whom I have ever witnessed them. Mean-while, I am gratified that she puts me on a level with the Vestal Virgin's house and the candy pillars: if I have as much charm for her, I cannot lack beauty.

And then, what about Louise? I looked down at that white precious letter and turned my thoughts, a little reluctantly, to the other problems it posed. Simone almost seemed to imply in it that Louise was no more dislocated than I was. It was odd that she had mentioned that sinister Shakespearean sonnet, which had come into my head the first time I heard that Louise had chosen lilies for her bouquet. I went over it again, as best I could.

> They that have power to hurt and will do none,
> That do not do the things they most do show,
> Who, moving others, are themselves as stone,
> Unmoved, cold and to temptation slow
> They rightly do inherit heaven's graces . . .
> Something something something . . .
> Lilies that fester smell far worse than weeds.

But Louise, of course, had the power to hurt and did it. Why, then, this aura of virginity? Was it simply a trick of profile?

The fact that Louise had been alone in that church disturbed me profoundly. Why wasn't she with her husband? I wasn't surprised, but I was disturbed. Indeed, I was so little surprised that the news seemed like a confirmation of something. Poor *elegantissima* Loulou, wandering sadly around Rome by herself looking at ancient monuments. Whatever Louise was now realizing, she must surely have foreseen: she wasn't stupid, nor was she carried away by idealistic fervours in marrying Stephen Halifax. Perhaps she was stoically realizing that she had miscalculated.

Re-reading Simone's letter again today, after an interval of months, I realize that there is nothing in it to suggest the betrayal and disillusion that I sensed.

I put the letter away, that evening, and tried to forget it, except of course for the charming sentiments about myself. After all, I said to myself, what had Louise and her marriage got to do with me? She was merely and accidentally my sister whereas Simone was a personal person of my own.

This is a lie, but a lie that I am often near to believing.

I now find myself compelled to relate a piece of information which I decided to withhold, on the grounds that it was irrelevant, but I realize increasingly that nothing is irrelevant. I meant to keep myself out of this story, which is a laugh, really, I agree: I see however that in failing to disclose certain facts I make myself out to be some sort of *voyeuse*, and I am too vain to leave anyone with the impression that the lives of others interest me more than my own. So I hasten, belatedly, to say that all this time that I have been writing about I was in love with somebody quite outside this story, so far outside it that thousands of miles separate him and it. His name is Francis. We were in love for our last year at Oxford, most inseparably in love. I felt as though he carried me around in his pocket. At the end of the year, our final year, he, being a great scholar, was awarded a Commonwealth scholarship to go and study political theory in Harvard. He said he wouldn't go. I said he should. I suppose we quarrelled.

I couldn't understand myself. Nothing could have appalled me more than the idea of his leaving me for a year, and yet I have never pursued any end with greater intensity. I think I suspected that half of him really wanted to go, and that he was determined not to merely through consideration of my feelings. I was equally determined not to be stayed with through anything but clear, unalloyed desire on his part. So, despite his fervent protests, I forced him to accept the scholarship and go to America. Perhaps he seriously didn't want to go. I long

73

since gave up any hope of knowing the truth about it. The fact is, he went. Oh, I have been over it a thousand times: the fact that he went meant that he didn't love me, the fact that I drove him to it meant that I didn't love him, and so on forever. The fact remains, and now it is all that remains.

It is only now, at the time of writing (or rather, indeed, rewriting) that it occurs to me that I may have been simply delaying the problem of marriage. In a way I'm surprised that I didn't marry him straight away, on leaving college, as Gill had married Tony. I was dimly beginning to formulate the idea that of all the many kinds of marriages, Gill's and Louise's represented some kind of extreme, and that both extremes were to be avoided. I hadn't in any case done what Gill had done: whether I was to do what Louise had done – whatever that is and was – remains to be seen. I don't think I ever would, not through any difference in character, but through the happy accident of having once been truly in love. In fact I suppose that I will marry Francis. I have always supposed so. It's unlikely that I could ever love anybody else. But don't take this as meaning that all was straight and tidy between us – all was on the contrary tears and separation, and I had never so much as mentioned the idea of marriage to my family. And, moreover, had I been never so happily engaged, all the problems of jobs and work and domesticity would have remained. The days are over, thank God, when a woman justifies her existence by marrying. At least that is true until she has children. So what did Louise think she was doing? Was she going to have a family? The prospect was impossible to contemplate, and I don't think it ever crossed my mind during all my speculations about her marriage.

I was finally pushed into embarking on this Francis explanation because I now have to describe a party which would have been quite different had my status been other than that of an unmarried attached girl. It was the sort of party that doesn't matter at all if one is with a man, but which can be very dangerous or very unpleasant if one goes alone. It was the sort of party that I had forgotten: I had grown so used to being taken everywhere that I had forgotten what it meant to be alone. I knew it would be ominous as soon as the invitation arrived. It wasn't a printed one: it was typed, in rather precious sloping typescript, and it said:

nov 10   10 llandorff gardens N.W.6
 david   ildiko   simon
  vesey   bates   rathbone
  at home 9 pm bottles welcome partners welcome.

On my invitation the message about bottles and partners had been crossed out, but David had scribbled underneath 'Do come, we're short of girls.' It looked, in fact, precisely the sort of party that one shouldn't go to alone unless feeling detached, tough, or lecherous, and I might have hesitated more than I did if I hadn't liked David Vesey so much, and if Gill hadn't had an invitation too. She was out when the post arrived, but I had collected hers with mine on my way in. I could see from Gill's envelope that it was addressed to both her and Tony – Mr and Mrs A. Slater, it said, with their King's Road address. Tony had clearly opened the letter, read it, stuck it up again with Sellotape and readdressed it. I decided to wait till Gill came in before I made my mind up whether to go or not, but in fact I already sensed that I would end up by going. I knew I would be there.

David Vesey is an Oxford friend, who had been working for two years on a big London daily: he is very amusing and very clever, tending towards the pedantic, though Fleet Street was on the way to curing that, I didn't doubt. He writes imitation-French novels in his spare time, all about pursuing ways of life to the absurd or the logical (it didn't seem to matter which, owing to some strange

Gallic confusion of terminology). He hasn't published anything yet but I'm sure he will, once he stops making all his characters commit suicide in the last chapter in order to prove the supremacy of unreason. No publisher could take that, but the rest is really very funny. I wanted to see him again: we hadn't met for about a year He had known Francis well, which seemed to lend a sanction to the whole occasion.

Both Simon and Ildiko were aspirant actors. Ildiko had appeared at the Arts once, and had done several TV plays, after leaving RADA the year before. Simon was more successful, and had just finished a reasonably-sized working-class part in a working-class play at the Royal Court. I knew them both very slightly, through David and one or two people in the BBC, and didn't dislike them particularly, though I never could understand why an egghead like David could live with such flashy people. I don't know, actors seem to be so obvious, as though looking like an actor were half the job of being one. Perhaps it is. A devotion to forms and ceremonies and darlings and anecdotes: what artist or poet would ever say they loved art galleries or literary cocktail parties in the infatuated way in which actors say they love the theatre?

However, I liked actors well enough to think the evening might be amusing. So when Gill came in I was prepared to put a little pressure on her to persuade her that she would enjoy it too. She didn't get back till late: I had spent the evening lying on the hearthrug smoking, reading a pile of scripts of appallingly touching rawness, and eating a pile of apples, so I suppose that what with ash, apple cores and sheets of typescript everything was rather a mess: but nevertheless I was unprepared for her opening words.

'For Christ's sake, Sarah,' she said, as she shook the rain primly off her umbrella all over the carpet, 'what an absolutely *filthy* mess. The place looks like a pigsty.'

I sat up, looked round, and replied vaguely and probably very irritatingly, 'Yes, I suppose that perhaps it does.'

'I don't know how you can *live* in it,' she pursued, proceeding to unbutton her plastic raincoat. I would rather drown than wear a plastic raincoat, and so would Gill have done in the old days. Desertion does funny things to a woman.

'Oh, it isn't too bad,' I said.

'It's absolutely filthy,' she said again, and went into the bathroom, dripping her raincoat and umbrella all the way. She looked so dreary, her face tight and disapproving, her hair all wet and plastered back under a head-square. I decided I'd better say something placating, but hadn't the energy, so I changed the subject, instead.

'There's a couple of letters for you, Gill,' I said, as she came back again, rubbing her hair with a towel.

'Oh, are there? Where?'

'On the mantelpiece.'

She read the first one very quickly, and then opened the invitation; as she took it in her expression clouded. She stood there scowling at it, then she looked down at me, read my face, and said, 'I suppose you've got one too?'

'Yes, I have,' I said. 'I haven't seen David for ages, have you?'

'No, I haven't, and I can't say I particularly want to.'

'Why, what's wrong with David?'

'Oh, nothing.'

'I thought I'd probably go.'

'What on earth for? It's bound to be an utterly sick-making drunken orgy, with foreign girls and models with their hair done up over bird-cages. And actors.'

She paused for my response, which didn't arrive.

'Well, isn't it?' she repeated aggressively.

'I don't know,' I replied. 'I suppose so. But I rather like that kind of person.'

'Well I don't. I think they're silly and tiresome and I should be bored to tears.'

As she said that, I suddenly glimpsed in her the traditional university woman, badly dressed, censorious, and chaotic. I didn't like what I saw, so I quickly said, 'I like David.'

'I do too, in a way, but he likes such silly girls.'

'Some men just do. One can't do anything about it, can one?'

'It annoys me, that's all, to see him getting intense about nitwits with their hair six inches high.'

'He doesn't get intense,' I said plaintively. 'He just likes girls. He can't help it.'

'When's his novel coming out, anyway?'

'I've no idea. Is there one on the way?'

'Well, isn't there?'

'Not that I know of.'

'He'll never publish anything if he goes on being a journalist. All he cares about is money.'

'Oh shut *up*,' I said, 'and stop getting at him for such stupid contradictory reasons. Why don't you want to go to this party, anyway? I thought it might make a change. We could go together.'

'A change from what?'

'Oh, you know. People in ties. Everyone will drink horrid wine like the good old days in Ox. Do come, I'd be scared to go by myself.'

She didn't respond to this moving appeal, but looked down again at the invitation with a puzzled look.

'I don't get it,' she said, after a pause, shaking her tidy damp head. 'I just don't get it. Look.'

She handed the piece of card over to me: it was exactly the same except that David had only crossed out the Partners Welcome message, and Tony had added underneath: 'I shall be there.' I looked from it to her to see what she didn't get, and she said, 'What does he mean? I don't know what he means.'

I thought hard and quick.

'Perhaps he's just telling you he'll be there so you can go too.'

'Do you think so?'

'Look, Gill, how should I know?'

'Perhaps he's warning me not to go? Which do you think, is he warning me not to go or expecting me to go and meet him there?'

'I really don't know,' I repeated, touched but a little embarrassed by her questioning: I didn't see how she could expect me to understand Tony if she didn't. I would never never ask anyone else about Francis. But Gill seemed genuinely to have resigned the right to know what Tony was doing. Obviously her surface neatness covered unpleasant depths of doubt. Still, despite my reluctance even to express an opinion about Tony, I was relieved that she had stopped pretending that the causes of her distress were the mess on the floor or the hair-styles of model girls.

'I should think that perhaps it means that he would like you to go,' I said, finally. I didn't really think so but I hadn't the nerve to suggest the other thing. 'When did you last see him?'

'It was at Beata's.'

'Was he pleased to see you?'

'Not really. He was with another girl.'

'What a lout,' I said. That seemed to clinch everything to me, though I still couldn't say so: after all, Tony is very odd and may well have wanted to meet his lost wife at David Vesey's party. But as she seemed inclined not to go, I couldn't in fairness discourage her from this inclination. She did persuade me, however, to go myself and to report on the state of affairs: who Tony was with, what he looked like, *etcetera*.

6 The Party

November the tenth was a strange and promising day. I woke feeling higher than I had done for the past week, which had been distinguished chiefly by an involved airmail confusion with Francis. I had been making difficulties to him, and I always hate myself for that, and at the same time feel an ominous horror because it is always a sign that I am about to have a crisis of malice, weeping and exhaustion. I had felt it coming for days: I had been crouching inside the walls of my consciousness terrified to move too far or too violently in case they collapsed and left me looking at the wild beasts. In the pre-crisis days I feel like someone living in a paper house surrounded by predatory creatures. They believe the house is solid so they don't attack, but if I were to move they would see the walls flutter and collapse and they would be on to me in no time.

But somehow, on the morning of that day, the crisis seemed averted. Perhaps it was quite simply that when I woke the sun was shining through the flimsy curtains on to my bed. And by the first post there came a letter from Francis that seemed to confirm the change in the weather: it said the only things that can comfort: it said, foolishly but beautifully, 'Beloved angel, I believe you whatever you say, even if it isn't true, because I believe you are true,' and so forth: it forgave me, *carte blanche*, absolutely, in that extraordinarily generous way that Francis has. And at the end of the letter he said, 'I know you must be extravagant, my lovely angel, I wouldn't have you clip your wings and put up with the common good of life, so burn the time away till nightfall.' I could have eaten the words on the page. He seemed more present than he had seemed at any moment since he had left, and as I walked out into the bright sunlight to catch the bus I could feel the wild beasts slinking away with their tails between their legs, balked of their rightful prey.

It was a wonderful blue cold day, with the last yellow leaves reprieved on the terrace of plane trees by the bus stop: almost one of those aqueous and lunar days when everything is charged with its own clarity. The colours of the houses and the brick were glowing and profound, and the small children playing in the streets looked as though they were on the way to an entrancing future. I had a good day at work, with a few odd compliments from above, and my good mood was still with me when I returned home in the evening to change for David's party. Deciding what to wear was a pleasure instead of the usual burden: I took down my dresses and skirts with an affectionate proprietary familiarity, and tried on this and that without once thinking that I looked a fright. In the end I put on an enchanting linen dress with pleats and a yoke, rather like a gym tunic, which I had bought two years ago, long before such things became fashionable. It was a wonderful and exhilarating dress to wear because it left me complete freedom of movement: it had no belt to sever my legs from the movement of my shoulder, it didn't mould or make me any way, it just met me where I went out to meet it, with a casual friendliness. It was a perfect garment to feel happy in. I hung a lump of amethyst on a silver chain which Simone had once given me round my neck, then looked for my lilac eyeshadow: I couldn't find it, so decided that eyeshadow was anyway vulgar. I spent five minutes putting my hair up, and then took it all down again. I thought I looked fine either way. Then I spent another ten minutes looking for the invitation with the address on it, which had slipped behind the clock on the mantelpiece. Then I decided it was getting very late, so I grabbed my coat and the first book I could see, and ran for the bus. I always take a book with me to parties, I find it is a girl's best chaperone, but I did wish I'd picked up something more likely than *Paradise Lost*.

To get to NW6 from N5 one has to go into Piccadilly and change. It took time, but I enjoyed myself looking out of the bus at the shop windows, which were all lit up in garish Christmas colours, red and green and tinsel and electric blue. Christmas Offers had begun to replace the cut prices. I loved it all, all the candles and the posters and the cold bonfire air.

When I got to David's the party was in full swing. I could tell that from the bottom of the stairs. They were rather cold, grey, office-like stairs. In fact they were office stairs: he and Simon live on top of an accountant's. There was a raucous noise descending – not the even, beelike murmur of cocktail conversation, but a much more extrovert, high-pitched roar, with a background of music and feet shuffling, from which an individual voice rose from time to time in a wail or shriek of gaiety. I took all this in, quietly, before I drew a deep breath, remembered that I was my love's lovely angel, and pushed open the door. I found myself in their crowded hall, full of smoke and heaps of coats and people. After the preliminary dazzle, I distinguished David with his back to me, so I made my way over to him and attracted his attention by shouting 'David' in his ear: he lurched round, scattering white wine all over the girl whose glass he had been filling, and said, '*Sarah*, I'm so glad you came. Wasn't it nice of you to come? There's a terrible scrum in here, isn't there?'

'Terrible,' I agreed, 'but it's just what I feel like.'

'Is it really? I've had enough. I wish they'd all go home. Except that would mean they hated my party and that would be too depressing, wouldn't it? So they'll all have to stay till morning.'

'They will, you needn't worry,' I said, looking round. Everyone looked very much settled down for the night. David himself appeared to be a little distraught and very hot: he kept trying to push the hair off his forehead with the back of the hand that was holding the bottle.

'What do you want to drink?' he said. 'There seems to be white wine, red wine or beer, and I believe there is some Scotch hidden in the kitchen cupboard. Or there was, once. Would you like some Scotch?'

'No thank you, really, I'd rather have some white wine, I hate Scotch.'

'Do you really?' he said, as he started off through the crowd to a table in the corner of the next room. 'I thought you used to be a hard drinker? Don't I remember you and Francis and me getting through a bottle or two?'

'Maybe,' I said, 'but times have changed.'

'Not for me they haven't.'

'Haven't they?'

'There, will that do?'

He handed me a half-pint beer-mug full of wine: 'Oh God,' I said, 'that's far too much, it looks so bad.'

'Well, you'll get through it, won't you? Are you drinking to talk or to get drunk, as Aristophanes once said to Socrates?'

'Did he really? You old pedant. To get drunk, I suppose. Not much chance of a conversation round here.'

'What do you mean? There's lots of intelligent people here. Lots of old friends. And how is Francis? He's a real pedant, old Francis.'

'Oh, he's all right. Who's here then that I like?'

'Don't you like everyone? What about Stephanie and

Michael? There they are, talking about H-bombs. Go and tell them not to be so worried.'

'All right, I will. Will they make me sign anything? I saw Stephanie on a newsreel the other day, handing out pamphlets at that to-do outside Brize-Norton.'

'Darling Stephanie, I wonder why she isn't a bore. She must see how absurd it all is. You go and talk to her, I must fly off and deal with the new arrivals. If I know any of them. Honestly, there are so many people here that I've never seen in my life before. Do you think they would gatecrash my parties if I wore glasses like Francis?'

'Of course they wouldn't,' I said, loudly, over the heads of people who started to surge between us: then I turned and made my way over to Stephanie and Michael. On the way I caught sight of Tony. He was dancing, in a very confined space, with a beautiful foreign-looking girl who was wearing an extraordinary bright yellow dress with a silk fringe round the bottom.

Stephanie and Michael were both very much from the old administration. They had been one of the steady couples in Oxford, with a predictable career mapped before them of three years' idyll followed by a July wedding immediately after Finals: all of which had, of course, charmingly happened. Stephanie had been my great stand-by just before exams: she had kept drifting into my room late at night, as I sat up with cups of coffee over volumes of *Beowulf* and the dead relics of past essays, bringing with her patterns for wedding dresses, scraps of material, and ideas for bouquets from *Vogue*. I discussed these things with her with much greater enthusiasm than I could summon up for eleventh-hour revision, and was sorry I missed her wedding through being in Paris. She wasn't at all a frivolous person, as that description of her might suggest: but then neither was she a real academic bore like me.

Both she and Michael are, separately and as a couple, the sort of people one might very much like to be, if one didn't suspect that through thus gaining nearly everything one might lose that tiny, exhilarating possibility of one day miraculously gaining the whole lot. Both their families were connected with professional politics, and they followed politics with the kind of committed, critical enthusiasm that others reserve for theatre reviews or literary fashions. They made political earnestness respectable in our circle, because of their evident soundness and intelligence, but somehow I could never go the whole way with them. 'It's no good,' Francis had said to me late one night after a long session on immigration from the West Indies. 'They believe people can be changed and I don't. That's basically what it is.' And I was with Francis on this point, not in a despairing Tory way, but because I do believe that people can't be changed: they can only be saved or enlightened or renewed, one by one, which is a different thing and not one that can be affected by legislation.

So when I went over to join Michael and Stephanie, and found them deep in Nuclear Disarmament with a junior civil servant and an unknown girl, I couldn't quite meet their fervour. 'Yes, I know,' I kept saying, as ever, when Stephanie turned to me for support, 'but what does civilization *mean*? What is it, exactly?' I was slow at grasping their concepts: for example, liberty, which means something very significant when applied to everyday life, means very little to me with reference to political institutions or secret police. After all, one is always free to be shot. Always. Which puts liberty, compromisingly, within. They didn't see it like that, and I'm sure I wouldn't have done had I been in a police state: moreover, as Stephanie used often to say, I am subject to subversive capitalist pressures from magazines like *Vogue* which make me want things I don't want. But I am still free not to buy them. Ah yes, says Stephanie triumphantly, but you're not free not to *want* them. And she has a point there, I can't deny.

I did very much enjoy seeing them again, and drinking white wine, and feeling moral concern and uplift. We exhausted the H-bomb, and passed on, *via* the death of culture, to whether people ought to keep works of art in their houses, or in museums for the whole world to enjoy: I was rather reluctantly Fascist about the problem, and kept saying annoying things like What do the Working Classes want with Botticelli. The other girl, who appeared to be an out-of-work friend of Ildiko's, was inspired by this to various utterances on the economics of the theatre, and we were just about to engage ourselves with the next absorbing series of problems (the Arts Council, state finance, the *Comédie Française*, the Moscow Arts) when Stephanie suddenly broke the circuit by an abrupt digression.

'Did you see,' she said to me, 'that picture of Louise in the *Tatler*?'

'Louise? No, what on earth was she doing in the *Tatler*?'

'Well, it was really about her husband, at some sort of conference in Paris. Didn't you see it?'

'No, I don't take the – '

'Neither do I, but I happened to see it at the doctor's. I forgot to tell you, Sarah, I'm having a baby. Or so the doctor says. Isn't that nice?'

She said this, blandly smiling her smooth English smile, as though she were announcing her plans for an impending holiday, and as I congratulated her I had a sudden pang about Gill, the tears and the turpentine, the horrible operation in the red plush room with the classic but suggestive nudes on the walls, and her sitting alone in the empty flat while Tony clutched a girl with a yellow fringed dress to his bosom. It was a slow tune, as Stephanie spoke, and I could see Tony at the other end of the room, swaying and nibbling the yellow girl's ear. He didn't even look sad and embittered, he looked as if he were enjoying himself. Some people are born to a smooth life, I thought, as Stephanie brushed the smooth, gleaming loop of hair from her cheek as she leant forward to tell me about what the doctor had said and what the baby would be called. She was incapable of falling in love with a man like Tony, and that was why she was safe. She would wear pretty maternity dresses and be an excellent mother. It made me want to cry, and I even felt the tears rising, tears for Gill and for Francis and for me and for the baby I might some day bear, which would be born of blood and sweat and tears or not be mine. To stop this awful inappropriate sequence, I turned back to Louise, once the subject of babies had been decently dealt with, and said that I had thought that she was still in Rome, and did the *Tatler* say when the conference in Paris had been.

'Oh, I think it was at the beginning of the month,' she said. 'Louise looked quite ravishing, in a coat without a collar and a wonderful fur hat. I couldn't believe it when I saw it. It said they were going to film *The Decline of Marriage.*'

'*Film* it?' *The Decline of Marriage* was Stephen's first novel, and as pretentious and clever as its title.

'That's what it says.'

'They can't possibly film it, it hasn't got a *trace* of a plot. It's totally unfilmable. Did they say who was making it?'

'I don't remember. It said that Stephen Halifax was working at the moment on the script.'

'He must be mad. It's gone to his head. Honestly, it really is a joke, the way I never hear anything about my relatives until the whole world knows.'

'You should read the *Tat.*,' said Stephanie.

'I suppose I should,' I said.

'Do I gather,' said the strange actress girl, 'that Stephen Halifax is your brother-in-law?'

'That's right,' I said, suddenly angry and embarrassed about it: it was all very well for Louise to make herself a living out of Stephen's novels, but I didn't see why I should be implicated, why I should be compelled to experience spurious and vicarious satisfaction on their behalf. I am far too conceited to take any true pleasure out of any such connexion.

'Oh,' she said, 'are you really? Then perhaps you might get me a part in this film.' I didn't think she was serious, but theatre people are so odd, and I believe she very nearly was: she went on, 'I think Sappho Hinchcliffe is playing the girl, and they want John Connell to play the man.'

'How on earth did you hear all this?' I asked.

'Oh, gossip. The grapevine. Everyone knows. John Connell wants to do it, but can't because he's under contract to the Watford people, and although the Happy Hours play is coming off in December he's still tied up with them for the next play they're putting on. So it's a question of whether or not they release him.'

'I see,' I said, though I didn't. I was getting more and more put out by all this talk of babies and sisters and Stephen, which weren't at all the chords I had meant to touch: I had meant to have a festive evening. The talk about art galleries had faded out, and I now realized that my heart hadn't been in that either, as it would once have been. Film talk with this girl threatened to prolong itself, and I felt boredom creeping up on me: I was very relieved when a quite charming journalist friend of David's, whom I had never met before, wandered over with the oblique but evident purpose of asking me to dance. I finished my half-pint mug of wine and accepted: I love dancing with attractive people that I don't know well, especially in confined spaces. Like being on Tubes and trains in the rush-hour, if the person next to one happens to think the same way.

He danced rather nicely, this writer man, and held me in an appreciative kind of way, and said he liked my dress: when the music stopped he got me a drink and I drank it, and then we danced some more. He seemed as pleased to get off with me as I was to get off with him, and yet he wasn't particularly troublesome and didn't touch anything that I hadn't for years known was there. We both drank rather a lot and talked about all the other people in the room. He said the yellow girl with Tony was a friend of David's called Beatrice, and that Tony had stolen her the week before: I said had David minded, and he replied, 'Oh no! he just shook his shabby head and put his hands deeper in his raincoat pockets.' This answer enchanted me completely, and I said, 'I adore you,' and he said, 'I'm so glad, I'm so glad, I adore you too,' and went on dancing. And when, at the end of the next record, he suggested going to sit somewhere I accepted. He seemed to know the terrain pretty well, and we ended up in David's bedroom, which was already occupied by several other couples lying on the floor and bed and chairs. My man was quite undeterred by the occupied look of the place, and went and sat down on the end of the bed, giving a great push at the red velvet-covered bottom of the girl next to him, and saying, 'Hey, shove up.' She did, surprisingly, which I thought terribly funny: indeed, I couldn't stop laughing. There wasn't much room, but we sorted ourselves out and lay quite comfortably in the end. I felt very sleepy. Nobody else was talking, but the room was filled with vague amatory noises. Nobody seemed to notice that we were laughing. Jackie got as far as saying that the girl next to us had very big hips, and when there was no response from her he pinched her bottom, and she pushed his hand languidly away as if a fly had settled on her. After the pleasant passage of an indistinct amount of time, when I was almost asleep, my friend said, 'Look, are you still awake? Shall we go and have another dance? I feel like death all of a sudden.'

'Fine,' I said, and staggered to my feet. He pulled me into the corridor, where the light of the thirty-watt bulb made me blink like an owl, and said, 'Just stand there and wait for me, will you?'

'All right,' I said, running my hands through my rumpled, sticky hair, and preparing to prop up the door till his return. I was very meek. When he got back we wandered back to the dancing-room, and as we shuffled round he remarked on the changing social *ambiance* of the party. 'It's all these actors,' he said. 'There were just the out-of-work ones before, but now all the superior ones with jobs are arriving.'

I realized the force of his remark when I looked round and saw John Connell standing in a corner with a tall, red-haired, pale kind of man, surrounded by a group of sycophants: he saw me, as we approached their part of the room, smiled with heavy charm, and said, 'Evening, Sarah. Evening, Jackie.' As we moved away once more, my partner and I exchanged looks: 'At school with me,' said Jackie briefly: 'Best man at my sister's wedding,' I as briefly returned, and was surprised by how irrationally and how nearly I had said 'He married my sister.' I kept directing odd glances at John for the next half-hour, not sure why he interested me so much, and I tried to picture him as the anti-hero of *The Decline of Marriage*. He was looking very self-assured, and I sensed that he was being rude to people and getting away with it: he was very much the biggest fish in the bowl. I had no intention of going to add my small words to the circle of dislike and admiration which success attracts, and I was distinctly surprised when he intercepted one of my glances and started over to the corner where Jackie and I were sitting, with our sour cigarettes, holding hot hands.

He stood before us, huge and dark like a colossus, shutting out all the dim red light from our corner. I felt like a child: the fact that I was on the floor and he standing put me at a disadvantage. I felt, literally, small.

'Are you dancing?' he asked me, 'or have you given up for the night?'

'I haven't given up yet,' I said, without presence of mind.

'Then do you mind getting up from there? Excuse us, Jackie.'

I rose to my feet, dazed by the shock treatment: my reactions were slow that night. I murmured 'Wait' at Jackie Almond, who sat there, apparently waiting: I felt as though a head boy or a lord of the manor had removed me by right of place from a fifth-former or a serf. The minute John took hold of me I began to regret my feebleness: I badly wanted to sit down, as I didn't feel at all steady on my feet, nor at all able to engage in conversation. Also I was soon busy detesting myself for the faint *frisson* that came from dancing with the best-known and in a certain style the best-looking man in the room. He managed to hold me far more aggressively and personally than my nice Jackie person, and seemed to crush all the movement out of me. I felt squashed in his grasp, squashed and angry. He wasn't even dancing properly, he was just ambling around with me. It was only after a couple of minutes that I realized he wanted to talk, not to dance. The first thing he said was, 'Well, I saw your sister last week.'

'Oh, did you?' I replied.

'Yes, I did. She was in Paris. With Stephen, still with Stephen.'

I couldn't say less than 'Oh?'

'Amazing, isn't it? An old sod like Stephen.'

I didn't know how to comment on this either: I sensed

danger on every side. I was subdued by the way he kept his hand hard on my back ribs, and pushed me ever so slightly backwards, so that I felt off balance and defeated.

'I went to see them,' John continued, 'because Stephen wants me to be in a film of his, called *The Decline of Marriage*. A very good title, don't you think?'

'They'll never call the film after the book,' I said, priding myself on a faint glimmer of conversational tactics. 'They'd never go for that in Kidderminster or Cheltenham.'

'He wants me to be in it,' said John, with a carefulness that made me realize with relief that he was as tight as I was, 'because I'm his oldest friend.'

'Is that the only reason?'

'Oh, he's very loyal, is Stephen. That's his other oldest friend over there, talking to your boy-friend. Wilfred Smee. Ever met Wilfred?'

'That is *not* my boy-friend,' I said, childishly. All the same, I located Wilfred: he was the pink, sandy-eyelashed man I had noticed with John earlier.

'Wilfred is very worried about Stephen.'

Wisely, I didn't ask why. I didn't even say, 'Oh?'

After another long pause, he said, 'Well, aren't you going to tell me what Louise is up to?'

'What do you mean, up to?' I asked, full of dim guesses and forebodings.

'You know what I mean.'

'No, I don't. I'd be the last person to know anything about Louise. I haven't seen or heard from her since she was married. And apparently you have.'

'I saw her last Sunday. I flew over.'

'Clever of you, wasn't it.'

'Not as it turned out. It was a failure. Not what I'd been given to expect at all. What's your big sister up to?'

'I've told you before, I don't know,' I said, acutely

uncomfortable under the open hostility that had broken out. I was totally out of control, and wondered if I was imagining everything. In the end, taking a little courage, I said, 'Anyway, what are you so interested for?'

'Don't you know?'

'No.'

'You look like her, in a way.'

'No I don't.'

'You do. Hard as nails, both of you.'

'Do you mind.'

I was hurt and offended, and moreover I had more or less guessed what he was talking about, though I had no desire at all to proceed any further. It was odd that I didn't immediately know all the facts, then, at once, because when I did finally see the whole thing it didn't come with a shock of surprise but much more with a shock of inevitable familiarity. Rather as though I had been told it before and tried to forget, so that when I saw it I could no longer evade my own foreknowledge. Like children finding out about sex: they are shocked, surprised, and yet oddly certain that it must be so, because they have always known the unbelievable truth. And so I must have known about John and Louise, from the moment when I met Louise on New Street Station on my way home from Paris.

'You do look like her,' he repeated. He let go of my hand and took hold of my chin with his fingers, pinching it hard and painfully, and tilting my face towards the light: but I had had enough of being bullied, and I pulled away and said, 'Just let go of me, do you mind, just let me alone.'

He released me, as he had to, as I was standing stock still and quite unmanoeuvrable. 'Thank you for the dance,' I said, and started off back towards Jackie Almond and Wilfred Smee. He followed, and I tried very carefully to walk straight: I felt red in the face from drink and I remembered Louise's lily-like bloom. Jackie looked like an old friend when I rejoined him. I was introduced to Wilfred Smee, but could hardly bring myself to be civil, not that I had anything in particular against him: he seemed more sensitive to my state than John, and shortly they both removed themselves, at his instigation.

I sat down on Jackie's knee, weak with relief. He kissed my arm for a few minutes, intermittently and absent-mindedly, and then said, 'Come on, I'll take you home.'

'I'm all right,' I said. 'I don't need taking.'

'I always take girls home after parties.'

'Do you?'

'Always.'

'Do you like doing it?'

'I suppose I must.'

He helped me to stand up, and led me into the hall. I was very glad he hadn't taken what I had said about going home alone seriously, as I didn't feel like being submerged in depression alone in the small hours. Also I wasn't at all sure how to get back to the flat, and was happy to shelve the problem. As it happened, there was no problem, as this man called Jackie Almond, whose virtues and uses had increased with my exhaustion, actually possessed a car.

'I don't believe it,' I said, as he opened the door and put me in. 'I simply don't believe it.'

'This is why I always take girls home from parties,' he said, pulling out the starter thing.

'Why? Because it's easy for you?'

'No. Because it's easy for them.'

This charming answer quite disarmed me: the old-fashioned, well-brought-up chivalry of him, together with the comfort of sitting in a warm car instead of walking the cold streets looking for non-existent taxis, effected a sag in the moral nerve that I had subconsciously braced to meet the cold and the walking: I had been ready to go home alone, on foot if need be, and the unexpected blessing of a car upset me. I started to cry. I felt terribly stupid, sitting there and crying: crying after parties is a habit I gave up at least a year ago.

'God, I'm sorry,' I said. 'How stupid of me. How stupid. It's just that I'm so glad I haven't got to walk.'

I was sniffing, as I always do when I cry, and I couldn't find my handkerchief, so he lent me his. It was almost like having Francis there.

'I get so terribly fed up,' I said, as I blew my nose, 'of being alone. I am sorry, please don't notice, I am sorry.'

I really meant it, too: there was a time when I would have cried really, I suppose, for attention, but this time I simply couldn't help it. More honourable, in one way, but more degrading.

'Most girls cry after parties,' he said, suddenly, as the car started forward in the dark.

'Do they?'

'Most of the sort of girls that I take home.'

'What sort are they?'

'You would be offended, wouldn't you, if I said your sort?'

I sniffed and hesitated, and then said, 'Yes, I suppose I would. One likes to be distinct, at least.'

'Even if it were the nicest sort of girl?'

'What sort is it then? Apart from being my sort?'

'Which you wouldn't recognize as a sort?'

'Not except as an insult.'

'Isn't there any sort I could say you belonged to that would please you?'

'I don't want you to please me. I want you to tell me what you mean.'

'Oh, of course. I understand that. But discounting what I mean, isn't there anything that would please you if I did say it?'

'If you said it and meant it, do you mean?'

'Of course.'

'No, I don't think there is. I don't want to be the sort of girl that you take home. Now tell me what you were thinking of.'

'Oh, nothing very much. You make the whole business sound rather terrifying, but then that's one of your qualities. You and your sort. The high-powered girls, I would call you. I like high-powered girls, particularly at parties. I like them all the time, but they never seem to like me.' He pulled a mock-pathetic face, which I think was rather serious, but I wasn't really thinking of him. I was thinking of me as a high-powered girl. For some reason the phrase didn't offend or threaten me, but seemed to say something true, something that connected up with me and how I had been, and moreover connected me with how other people were. It was this last connexion that really mattered: it expressed one quality of living that I would really like to have. I would like to be high-powered, in a way that I wouldn't like to be or to be called Bohemian, or bourgeois, or intellectual, or promiscuous, or any of the other charges that I had laid myself open to. I was, in a way, all these things, I suppose, but I didn't belong to them. I only belonged to them relatively, depending on who was watching: Daphne, Francis, Louise, David Vesey . . . But to being high-powered I hoped I did belong, and he had caught me in a pattern of behaviour that I would like to hold to, he expressed my community with people that I would like to belong to, people like Simone and Gill and one or two others that I have met. His words seemed to dispel a little of the isolation of behaving as I do, a little of the classlessness and social dislocation that girls of my age and lack of commitments feel. I sat silent, amazed by the recognition of how much I missed community, and how deeply I felt my social loneliness. I had no colleagues, no neighbours, no family.

After a while he said, 'Well? Why do you think they

don't like me?' and I realized that he had of course been thinking of himself.

'I'm sure they do,' I said. 'If I am one, they do.'

'Do you really?'

'Of course I do. Why did I spend the evening with you?'

'Convenience?'

'Did you spend it with me for convenience?'

'No, I did it because I like girls like you. I like you.'

'And I did because I like men like you. Chivalrous men.' He winced at that, but what could I say? 'Anyway,' I went on, 'I'm sure all high-powered girls must like you, out of self-defence, because so few people will put up with them. There aren't many people I could meet at a party who would put up with the whole lot from me, drink and bad dancing and weeping on the way home and all. One must be grateful.'

'Oh, one must. I suppose I must be grateful that girls need this kind of attention.'

'Yes. And there we are.'

'Mutual gratitude.'

'That's right.'

'You don't think that's rather sordid?'

'Not really. Why should it be?'

He didn't reply to this and I drifted off again on a private tack: I was thinking that despite all, despite the dislocations that made this sort of contact so necessary in its ephemeral way, the contact itself was worth it. Driving along a street I'd never seen with a man I'd never met in the dark of considerable understanding was worth a lot of the rest of life. I am never really happy unless lost in this way, and connected in this way. It's not that I don't like playing social games: I enjoy playing at cashmere cardigans or First Nights, or superior restaurants, or literary teas, or jazzy nightclubs, but while playing these things I never have any sense of connexion with the other people doing them, and am always more aware of the event making me than of me making the event. Whereas now, alone in the dark with this man, who assuredly didn't mean anything permanent to me, nor I to him, I felt liberated, as though I were drawing a little on his energy and he on mine. I don't know what I am missing in my life of permanent and valuable contact, though I feel its absence, but at least from time to time I get something that I would never get were I not so displaced – the sudden confidence, the momentary illumination of feeling, ships passing and moreover signalling in the dark.

It's all compensation, I suppose. But then I wouldn't have most of the things that it's compensation for. Excepting Francis. And who knows, respecting Francis I sometimes think I may be able to have my cake and eat it.

He took me home, and I remember that we shook hands on parting. I wanted to ask him in for a drink, but I knew what would happen if I did so I didn't, after a little thought. I felt bad, shaking hands like that.

In bed I remembered that John had said Louise and I were alike. I wondered how right he was. It needed considerable discernment to see that we resembled each other at all.

7   The Next Invitation

I had a bad time explaining about Tony to Gill the next evening. It didn't seem helpful to say that he was well and happy, as though I had visited him in hospital. What I did say was that I had scarcely spoken to him, and that he had been dancing with a friend of David's called Beatrice.

'What was she like?' said Gill, sitting on the floor and biting the quick of her nails.

'She had a horrid yellow dress on,' I said.

'Really horrid?'

'Yes, really horrid.'

'He likes such awful people,' she said.

We spent a horrible evening, somehow typical of the temporary pointlessness of our lives: we listened to the wireless, and I tried to write to Francis. I then made us both a curry, which I thought was rather kind and un- selfish of me, but Gill was furious when I put an iron casserole with rice in it on the coffee-table: she said it would burn a hole: I said so what, it wasn't our table: she said she didn't like looking at tables with holes burned in them: I said since when: she called me an undergraduate: I called her an undergraduate: and so on. I ended up feeling utterly childish and worn out, as though I weren't old or disciplined enough to live without support, and so I went to bed. Girls shouldn't share flats, but who else can they share them with?

The whole of the next month went on in the same way, cluttered up with intractable material objects like dirty saucepans and shoes that needed new heels, and although

I didn't get any tidier I began to share Gill's irritation with everything in the flat. I was relieved to get out to work in the mornings.

The next thing that happened was an invitation from Louise. It arrived at breakfast-time on a Saturday morning in late November. I hadn't heard anything of her since John Connell's elliptic comments at David Vesey's party: nobody seemed to have seen her, so I had assumed she was still in Paris. The invitation was for an 'At Home' at six-thirty on December the seventh. I was rather shocked by the unfamiliar, printed self-assurance of the words 'Mr and Mrs Stephen Halifax'. She really had done it. There was a note in with the invitation: it said –

24 Honeyman Gardens, SW3

My dear Sarah,

O to be in April now that England's here. We seem to have returned to the rain of the whole year: we would have stayed, but for Stephen's film, which I expect you know of. Do come to this party and look at our pretty flat.

Amitiés sincères, as they say in France,

Loulou

I read and re-read this communication several times as I chewed over my cornflakes: it seemed surprisingly amiable, but I was so well-trained in suspicion that I searched for *doubles entendres*, the iron hand beneath the velvet glove, and so on. The sad thing was that, as always upon renewed contact with her after a gap of time, ninety-five per cent of me leaped forward, earnest and happy to greet any sign of friendliness: I did still *want* to like her: but the other five per cent had been so often proved right that it was getting increasingly hard to confuse. On the face of it her letter seemed to be friendly enough: in fact it seemed too friendly to be normal. We never corresponded unless we wanted something from each other, and we never invited each other to anything.

Doubtless there *are* sisters who immediately rush to see each other after returning from abroad, and doubtless there are even more sisters who, if having a party, would invite each other to it as a matter of course, but we didn't belong to either of these groups. It never occurred to us to approach each other. I had assumed that when she returned to London the sum of our contact would be odd meetings in shops, art galleries and coffee-bars, sometimes civil and sometimes not, occasionally prolonged into cups of coffee or drinks together, but more often not. This had been the pattern of things in our frightful year together at Oxford, and I hadn't seen any reason why it should be changed. I wouldn't have dared to change it myself: I had thought to avoid her even more insistently now she was married.

It hadn't always been like this, of course: there had been a time when, happily oblivious of my own undesirability, I had pursued her and waited on her and yearned for the crumb of her company that never fell my way. This had lasted from the age of eight until I was thirteen or so: before I was eight she used to play with me quite often, and after the age of thirteen I learned at least superficially to ignore her and to get on with my own life. But the humiliating period after she had cast me off and before I learned to appear to have cast her off I remember very clearly. Particularly I remember the ends of term, when she would come home from boarding school, while I was still going to the local girls' school: I would cross the days off on my calendar for the last fortnight of term with growing excitement, and when the day came I would beg my parents to take me to Birmingham station with them to meet the train. They always did, touched by my enthusiasm, and I would stand on the platform counting the minutes till the train came in. When it was late I nearly died of suspense.

I always had a lot of fascinating things to tell her and

fascinating questions to ask her about school and her friends there. And every time she came there would be the same cold disillusion, the same sharp lesson in withdrawal. I remember her walking down the platform with her brown suitcase and her green school coat and hat, oddly detached from her school-friends, who were jabbering and giggling under the strain of meeting their families in full view of each other. No doubt she was even more selfconscious than they were, but by the age of thirteen she had learned not to show it. She would walk slowly and carefully, deliberately avoiding any appearance of haste: when she was within speaking distance a cool embarrassed little smile would cross her face. She would kiss my parents calmly, without fuss, rather as though they were strangers, and she would not look at me at all. Not once, ever. She ignored my existence completely.

Perhaps, looking back on it, I was a distinct social encumbrance. Mama and Papa looked quite reasonable, even though Papa was only a businessman (a fact which later caused her great concern), but I looked like the typical little sister, scruffy, eager and dirty. My hair used to be in horrid little plaits which didn't really work, and my shirts always escaped from my skirt waists. Doubtless in the brave show of independence and maturity which Louise managed to assume even below a school hat and amidst other uniformly hatted girls I was an almost insuperable humiliation. So I was ignored. I never understood why she wouldn't talk to me, and all the way home in the car as we sat together on the back seat I would volunteer my scraps of information about the cat's latest litter of kittens or our sickly and aged dog, but they never aroused any spark of response. I couldn't believe that she wasn't interested, so I went on telling her, though I wasn't insensitive to her blankness: I suppose I was wound up to such a pitch of expectancy that I had to let it out somewhere. It usually took me only a day or two to swallow the disappointment, and to learn to leave her alone. I would stop knocking on her bedroom door and trying to talk to her when she was reading.

I make myself sound pathetic, and I was. But she mishandled me: with a little skill or duplicity she could easily have persuaded me to run errands for her. Many other little sisters I knew or have since known were reduced to an inconspicuous, subservient position by a little tact. Perhaps Louise, by being openly sadistic, was merely being honest. At least she allowed me, by her manner, to salvage my dignity after a year or two, for I turned on her in the end. I used to laugh at her with my school-friends, to borrow her clothes without asking, and to steal her books. Once I read her diary. She would have read mine, had I kept one. In the end she taught me the art of competition, and this is what I really hold against her: I think I had as little desire to outdo others in my nature as a person can have, until she insisted on demonstrating her superiority. She taught me to want to outdo her. And when, occasionally, I did so, her anger hurt me, but as I had won it by labour from indifference, I treasured it. And when, finally, I took over one of her men at Oxford, the game was out in the open, I thought, for the rest of our lives.

And yet I don't want to imply that we never met on any grounds at all. In many ways we have much more in common than most sisters have: our interests, our intelligence, our paths through Oxford have been remarkably similar. In fact, in everything that is personal and not generic we tend to agree. There is just this basic antipathy, this long-rooted suspicion, that kept us so rigorously apart. And at times, talking of a book or a place or a person, we would be in sympathy. At times.

So the tone of her letter was really nothing new: we had quite a lot of shared jokes, of the sub-literary kind, consisting of allusions and vocabulary and suchlike. It was just that, somehow, I hadn't expected to hear from her at all. And in spite of myself, in spite of all the mechanism of suspicion that had been set in motion. I was pleased. I wanted to tell Gill, so I picked up my cup of Maxwell House and went into the kitchen where I could hear her banging about. I'd thought she'd been cooking herself some breakfast, but found she was doing the washing-up from the night before. This annoyed me because, although I'd no idea of the time, I knew that she was due to leave for work, and we had always said that she was to leave everything for me at the weekends, as I didn't work on Saturdays. I tried to tell from her manner whether she was being martyred or not, and decided from the way she banged the plates into the plate rack that she probably was.

'I've had an invitation from Louise,' I said.

'Lucky you,' she said, and removed the saucer from under my cup of coffee and started to wash it up.

'I didn't know she was back,' I continued, peaceably.

'Didn't you?' she said, and tipped all the cutlery into the washing-up bowl at once with a great splash.

'Look,' I said, 'what on earth are you doing all that for? You know I always do it on Saturdays.'

'I know you always say you will.'

'Well, I always do, except for last week when I had to go out. And even then there was no need for you to do it, I hadn't forgotten.'

'How was I to know you hadn't forgotten? When you come in in the evening and find everything just as it was at breakfast, you assume it's been left.'

'You knew perfectly well I wouldn't leave it for you.'

'I don't care who you leave it for, you can't expect me to come in and sit down with all that mess lying around.'

'Why on earth not? There's no need to sit in the kitchen and stare at it, is there? You could go in the other room and shut the door.'

'You may be able to. I can't.'

'You should always be able to shut the door on things.'

'That's what you call repression,' she said.

'No it's not. It's you that's suffering from repression. Or compensation. Or something unhealthy. It's simply morbid not to be able to forget the washing-up.'

'I think it's morbid to leave it there lying around.'

'Why? Just tell me why?'

'It's so messy. So uncivilized. And you have to do it in the end so why not do it before it starts to look such a disgusting mess? The egg dries on, too.'

She reached for the wire pan-scrub, and started to scrub the remainder of last night's omelette from one of the forks. The sight of it was too much for me: for one thing, I can't bear to use a pan-scrub myself, except the sort with handles, because the feel of the wire and the washing-up water really makes me miserable, and yet there was Gill, washing up my plates without a trace of squeamishness, while I was attacking her for being sensitive to mess. For another thing, the cutlery happened to belong to me: it was a birthday present from my parents, and I was fond of it. It had wooden handles, and was very beautiful, not like that deformed and embryonic Swedish stuff, and I felt defensive about it because I had asked for it with the conscious thought of having it ready for when Francis and I got married. And yet if anyone had asked if we were going to marry, I would probably have said No. It was the accumulation of these false positions that made me shout at Gill, although I had fully intended to be forbearing, and had indeed been treading gently for weeks. 'For Christ's sake,' I said, 'stop nagging and complaining at me, you're absolutely impossible to live with, I'm surprised Tony put up with it so long, and don't you know that you shouldn't put knife handles in water. They're absolutely ruined from the way you keep washing them. I'd rather they never got washed at all.' I wished I hadn't as soon as the words were out of my mouth; she didn't turn round at all but went quietly on to the next fork. I looked at the neat, work-tidy nape of her neck, and felt tears of shame rising to my eyes, and of regret for the evenings in college when we would sit amongst the cigarette ash and coffee-cups to talk about free, unencumbered things like people and paintings and stupid girls in hall. I was trapped and hopeless, and couldn't think how to say the fault was mine and Francis's, not hers and Tony's, when she suddenly said, 'Oh God, Sarah, what on earth are we going to do.'

'I don't know,' I said. 'I don't know at all.'

'It's hopeless. Utterly hopeless. If I'm like this with you what must I be like with other people?' She turned round from the sink, and I could see that she too was on the verge of tears.

'It's not your fault,' I said. 'It's my fault, I promise you it's my fault.'

'That's what I tell myself, but I don't convince myself. I tell myself, how on earth can Sarah be like she was when she's worried to death about Francis, and being lonely, and what she's going to do with herself, but I still feel it's my fault that you're how you are, and that you'd be better if you were living with someone else, instead of me being worried myself all the time . . . you know what I mean, you seem to treat me as though I were an invalid, you never talk to me straight out as you used to, and I have to keep reminding myself that it's because you're anxious yourself, not because I'm not worth talking to any more . . . you know, you never tell me about Francis or how he is or how you're getting on without him, and when I try to talk to you or ask you about Tony you cut me off as though I were a widow rambling about the dead. He's still alive, you know. He's still alive. But when I ask you to help me believe that he's still alive, and that there's still hope, you kind of politely change the subject.' All this while she had been twisting a tea-towel in her hands: now, with a sigh, she dropped it and finished with, 'You're so bloody tactful, Sarah, that's what it is.'

'It's because I was frightened of hurting you,' I said.

'Hurting me? I don't mind being hurt. I don't mind what you do to me, or Tony, or anyone. But I can't bear to be ignored. You can't treat me as though I were some other person who wasn't married to Tony and who hadn't gone and murdered their baby . . . no, I know what you're going to say, I know it isn't murder, I couldn't care less about abortions in fact, but nobody can take their own line the whole time without weakening at all, and there were days when I wanted you to tell me that it didn't matter, and that the things I thought were just the inevitable things that happen to anyone's mind . . . one night I dreamed I had had it after all, and I'd put it down somewhere and lost it, and it was time to feed it and it would be dying of starvation, and I looked and looked, and couldn't find it, though I could hear it crying and crying with hunger. . . I know it doesn't matter, dreaming things like that, but it *seems* to matter. Because I have nothing else to care about. Like the washing-up seems to matter, although I know I'm being an idiot about it . . . don't think I can't remember eating off the floor, and having six sour half-pints of milk on the mantelpiece, I do remember but it only makes it worse, the fact that I have to notice it now. All the dirt. And I thought you would understand things, because it was so marvellous to talk to you that day at Louise's wedding, but somehow you only make it worse, because you remind me so much of everything . . . you know what I mean?'

I did know too exactly what she meant. I was overjoyed that she had somehow broken through into speaking to me, despite the barriers that I had raised, or that had raised themselves between us.

'It's so terrifying,' I said. 'I thought you were so

resilient. And I suppose that I was scared to death on my own account when I found that you weren't, entirely. I felt to myself, if that happens to her, what on earth will happen to me?'

'I felt you feeling it,' she said. 'That wasn't very encouraging, either. It was rather like being one of those dead birds that farmers hang in fields to scare the live ones away.'

'How frightful I must have been,' I said.

'And me too. I still am, I suppose. What time is it?'

I looked at my watch and said that it was ten past nine. 'Then I'm late for work,' she said, 'but I don't suppose it matters. Yesterday I would have died rather than have been late. But it doesn't seem to matter now. Tell me about Francis.'

'Surely you ought to go?' I said, anxiously, and she laughed, and said, 'Honestly, Sarah, the joke is that you're just as bad as me. You're just as worried about being late and burning holes in landladies' carpets as I am, but you can't bear me to know it, so you always have to take the other side. Don't tell me you don't mind doing two days' washing-up when you get in late at night . . . I know you do, you always lose your temper quite ferociously, and that's why it annoys me so much when you take this moral line about not bothering about sordid things, leaving them till tomorrow, being late if you want to be, and all that nonsense . . . oh, I know it's right, I know it *is* the moral line, but you can't believe in it all the time yourself either, like the Catholics or whoever it is and God. You just pretend you don't have any lapses of faith. That's all it is.'

'You're right,' I said. 'Of course. And I'll tell you about Francis when you get back. But I really wanted to tell you about Louise.'

'So you did,' she said, beginning to put on her coat. 'You came in full of Louise, and I shut you up like a clam, and here I've been going on at you about not telling me things. Isn't it strange how in this kind of thing everything seems to be its own opposite? You know what I mean?'

Again, I did know what she meant, and the joy of having had so many intelligible things said to me during one morning sustained me for the rest of the day. Odd that one doesn't mind being called insensitive, selfish, and so on, provided that one can entirely understand the grounds for the accusation. It should be the other way round; one should not mind only when one knows that one is innocent. But it isn't like that. Perhaps the rare and simple pleasure of being seen for what one is compensates for the misery of being it. Anyway, the thought that Gill saw my failings more or less straight kept me happy for quite a while, and I didn't get round to remembering Louise until I went to bed that night, when I decided that for curiosity's sake I was at least justified in going to her party.

The next day I met Daphne in the Tate. I was somewhat surprised to find myself there anyway, and even more surprised to find her. It was Sunday, of course: Sunday is one of those days on which I expect to do typical, characteristic things – characteristic of myself, that is – yet usually end up doing things I don't want to do at all, going to places I know I'll loathe, and so on. This was a particularly bad patch: I seemed to spend my time seeing people I didn't care about, and talking about things that interested me only in a mild journalistic way. I never saw anyone who could arouse a flutter of apprehension and excitement, and who would turn out unexpectedly, and I couldn't think of anyone that I really wanted to see more than anyone else. Except Tony, but I couldn't look for him. And I wouldn't have minded seeing Jackie Almond, but I knew he was looking for a girl, and it hardly seemed fair to go and occupy him (as I sometimes felt I could quite easily have done) when I only wanted a little excitement and a little company. Perhaps I was too scrupulous about him, but I think not.

So the friends I did continue to see were of that odd, persistent variety that one sees largely through habit, and because they always have an address and telephone number. I can see that in a few years they will turn into the *genre* of 'friends of the family', and recur, sending the children Christmas presents and remembering my birthday, while those one passionately loved and wanted are swept into oblivion. Also, I saw a few people I had once cared about, but who were now too involved in their work or their wives or husbands to care about me. It was one of these who took me to the Tate – a chirpy historian by the name of Lovell, who had invited me to lunch with various academic cronies of Francis's, for old times' sake. It was a nice thought, and a nice lunch, but it made me feel curiously passé, and I felt the impulse to tell everyone that I had got a degree too, as good as any of theirs, which is always a danger signal. I resisted it, but it was sad to feel that way at all. Lovell was so nice and so friendly and so full of himself, and kept asking healthy unguarded questions about Francis, and telling me about his thesis, so I should have felt happy. But I didn't, I felt as though everyone else was leading a marvellous, progressive life except me, and that I had been subtly left behind. He didn't seem to notice, and it wasn't that I was exactly bored by the exhibition we had gone to look at; it was just that I simply didn't care, although I wanted to. I was bullying my brain and eyes to wake up and take a little interest as we stood in front of a charming sculpt of a little girl, when I suddenly noticed Daphne, my cousin Daphne, whom I hadn't seen since Louise's wedding. She was walking round the gallery alone, looking so like herself and what she was that she seemed a cross between a symbol and a cartoon. She was wearing a maroon coat with a fitted waist, and brown middle-height high-heeled shoes with thick heels; her hat was dark green and felt, and her handbag was rather expensive crocodile skin. Under the coat I could see she was wearing her Sunday suit and a pale blue blouse. She was carrying a string bag with a newspaper in: I was surprised they hadn't made her leave it at the desk. They must have recognized her transparent honesty. Once I was even made to leave my handbag – admittedly rather a vast one – solely because I had gone out in the morning without doing my hair or trying to put it up. If one could learn to put one's hair into the curious roll that Daphne wears, they would never ask to look at one's ticket again.

I wondered for a moment or two whether to notice her before she noticed me: I wasn't any too happy about the idea of introducing her to Lovell, who tended towards the satiric rather than the charitable. It was so obvious that I couldn't avoid her altogether, however, that I decided I had better salve my conscience and take the first plunge, though I went and ruined my moral vantage by whispering in his ear, before I hailed her, 'Just look at this too extraordinary cousin of mine, Charles.' 'Where?' he said, and I said, 'There,' and shouted 'Daphne' at her intent back. She turned round, recognized me, and came over looking chatty and not half as embarrassed as I was. I introduced her to Lovell, saying he was a friend of Francis's, and doing research at one of the London colleges: 'Oh,' she said brightly, 'you must be a historian, that's my line of country as well,' and I remembered that she was, in effect, a history teacher. She didn't look unlike a certain type of clever research student herself. But emphatically not Lovell's type: he liked clever women, but he only liked the smart and breezy sort in clever clothes who sit in libraries over a pile of learned books radiating successful control of mind and body and expensive feminine perfume. Anyway, Daphne wasn't even clever.

It turned out that she had come up to London for the weekend to attend some conference about marking School Certificate papers. I felt we ought to ask her to have a cup of tea with us, and was very grateful to Lovell when he suggested it himself: so we all trouped off to the restaurant and drank tea and talked about the paintings and history and other innocuous subjects. I was surprised by Daphne's *savoir-faire* in keeping off family gossip, and relieved by the small amount of work I was expected to do to keep the conversation going: she and Lovell seemed to have a lot to say about education, jokes in exam papers, *etcetera*. They got on to his thesis, and it wasn't until I heard Daphne say brightly and somehow desperately, 'It sounds absolutely wonderful, I'd love to hear some more about it sometime' that I realized she was actually, as they say, making a pass at him. He replied, 'Oh, I'll send you a copy when it's finished,' and I thought the time had come for interference.

'How's Michael?' I said, a little abruptly, as though I had just remembered his existence.

'Oh, he's all right,' she said and we turned the conversation to his holiday in Paris. After a while she politely and reciprocally asked after Louise. I was wondering how on earth I could convey to Lovell the fact that I wanted to break up our little tea-party, when she suddenly said she had to catch a train that evening up to the Midlands, and ought to be on her way to the station: she seemed determined to go by taxi, despite our advice about buses and Tubes, so we took her down the steps while Lovell performed the indelicate operation of waving at a taxi-driver. We shut her into the taxi, and she said as she left, pink with unexpected pleasure, 'I'm so glad I met you both, I really didn't know what to do with myself alone in London for a day.'

'You should have rung me up last night,' I said, but it wasn't me that had pleased her. She drove off, holding her string bag and her little suitcase as she sat there on the taxi seat, as though she were afraid the taxi-driver might turn round and grab them if she put them down for a second. In trains, she would never leave anything on the luggage rack. She had to take everything along with her to the restaurant car or the lavatory. And I'm sure she went in taxis because she was frightened of getting lost.

I don't know quite what I expected Lovell to say when she had gone. I didn't really think he would turn on me and say, 'What ghastly relations you have, I really can't associate with you any more if I'm liable to meet people like that in your company.' What he did say was, 'Poor girl, what a ghastly life it must be, teaching history from the sabre-toothed tiger to the Entente Cordiale.'

'She needn't do it if she didn't want,' I said tartly, spurred on to attack since he defended.

'What else could she do?'

'I don't know. Anything. Anyone can do anything.'

'In theory, perhaps. I must say it was a curious colour-scheme.'

'Very curious.' I looked at his delicately narrowed trousers, his expensive suède jacket, and his pretty green tie. 'Don't you think she could do better if she tried?' I said.

'Why should she try? It wouldn't help,' he said, and because it was cold standing on the steps there we started to walk off down the Embankment towards Lambeth Bridge. It was a very grey day and the river looked hopeless and beautiful, having given up autumn for dead and with as yet no thought of spring. It feels open down by the Thames in that reach, with the smell of traffic and estuary and barges. As we walked, a little speedboat passed us: in it I could see a man in a sheepskin coat, and a girl in a head-square hanging on to his arm as the wind blew in her face, and laughing. You can do that, even on the greyest, dirtiest stretch of river. It made me feel stagnant and covered in oil and dead feathers, to see them there.

Daphne is somehow a threat to my existence. Whenever I see her, I feel weighted down to earth. I feel the future narrowing before me like a tunnel, and everyone else is high up and laughing.

8 The Next Party

As the day for Louise's party drew near, I realized I hadn't got anything suitable to wear. There was no question of gaily and obliviously wearing something old and becoming like the linen dress I had worn to David's: I would have to make the effort of assessing the situation and finding something socially correct. I couldn't possibly afford anything new, being nominally at least self-supporting, and beyond writing to my father for a cheque, and yet I couldn't face going to see Louise in all her newly-married splendour without making some attempt to look appropriate. There wasn't a single six-thirty dress in my wardrobe, apart from a dreary black number that I had bought at the age of eighteen, when I first went up to college, under the impression that black was sophisticated. I suppose it is, but not on me. It makes me look drained and sallow. I think that if the dress problem had been straight in my mind I would have rung Louise up for a little mild chatter about Rome, but I never got round to it. In the end I asked Gill if she could lend me anything, and we spent a happy hour trying on each other's clothes: it was no use, because she was just slightly bigger in all directions than I was, and such garments as didn't mind being too big were far too arty for the occasion. Also, they were all very dirty. Cleaning is so expensive. I was about to resign myself to wearing the dreary black, which Louise had hinted to be a mistake almost on its first appearance, when Gill said, 'Why not try Stephanie? She's about your size – anyway, her things used to be too tight for me when

I used to try to borrow them. She's pregnant now, she won't want them any more.'

It seemed a brilliant suggestion, so we rang up Stephanie. She sounded delighted to hear us and asked us both round for a drink. We went, and there she was, sitting on a late Georgian settee knitting a blue pram rug and reading copies of *Vogue* and *Mother-to-be*. Her flat was beautifully furnished yet managed not to look opulent: she and Michael tended to believe that *objets d'art* ought to be kept in art galleries for the use of the public, so those that they had collected were discreet, almost austere. She was very helpful about the dress problem, and produced armfuls of suitable-looking things. She was obviously exactly the sort of person I should try to imitate for the occasion. I decided on a charming little dress in a sort of olive green, which made me look very unlike myself, but not altogether unconvincing. As we left, I was rather saddened and impressed by her ménage, but on the step outside Gill said, 'It's rather cosy, don't you think,' and, truly, I agreed. Gill is always tougher than me about other people. Sometimes I think I admire too much whatever I have not got. It's better than sour grapes, but Gill's reaction wasn't sour grapes either. She simply didn't want to live like that. Under the circumstances, she was lucky to know it.

The dress gave me a certain superficial confidence about the party, and I dressed for it not totally without pleasure: I had promised myself that I would go in a taxi, I suppose in order to feel more like the other guests and more like the dress I was wearing. Anyway, one gets so ruffled, walking in the cold and the wind. I worked it out so that I should arrive fairly late, and I was trying to pretend that I wasn't frightened as the thing drew up outside the white wedding-cake façade of their house, but when I over-tipped the driver and hadn't the nerve to ask for my money back, I knew that I was really in a bad way. I knew

I would have felt a lot better if I had asked for the change, but I didn't, even though there was time. After he had driven off with his undeserved two shillings, I took a deep breath, straightened my back, and started to walk up the few steps to the front door. At that point I would have given anything for my self-discipline to have allowed me to retreat and go home. But it didn't: retreat is about the last thing it ever allows me. When I reached the front door I faced another dilemma – I didn't know whether or not to ring the doorbell. There was a row of four bells, and Louise's was the next to the bottom: she lived on the first floor, obviously. In the end, after much deliberation, and spurred on by the awful thought of being caught hesitant on the doorstep by the next guest, I decided against ringing and walked straight in. I was reassured as soon as I was inside the door by party noises coming down the stairs: at least I hadn't fulfilled the worst of my nightmares and come on the wrong day. The noises, however, were ominous; there was no sound of any particular gaiety, only a subdued, indistinct, conversational hum. Clearly I was going to have to talk. Pulling the torn shreds of my arrogance more tightly around me, and hoping I didn't look as naked as I felt, I walked up the stairs and found another doorbell with Halifax by it, which I rang. This must have been the right thing to do, because Louise herself opened the door, and had obviously been standing in the hall waiting to do so. It was such a shock to see her that I had nothing to say.

She too looked taken aback, though not in any obvious way: 'Why, Sarah,' she said, very loudly, 'how enchanting to see you, how very kind of you to come.'

'How very kind of you to ask me,' I said.

'It must be months since I last saw you.'

'It is. It was September.'

'Oh yes, September. It was at my wedding, wasn't it?'

'That's right. At your wedding.'

'It seems a long time ago.'

'Yes, it does, doesn't it?'

We then paused a little to take breath in this scintillating exchange. She was looking very marvellous by any standards, wearing a kind of creamy-coloured wool dress in a curious towelling texture, neither knobbly nor hairy but a mixture of both. Perhaps it was more off-white than cream. It was obviously Italian, and my first thought was that she had obviously bought it in one of those fearfully worldly shops that I and my friends used to pass, dusty and more or less barefoot, clutching our bottles of wine, maps, postcards of irresistible objects like the bust of Augustus, and encumbered with all the weariness and useless cockleshells of pilgrimage. It gave me a strange feeling, to realize that a sister of mine had crashed into that other Rome, the Rome of the Romans. I decided some minutes later that perhaps, horror of horrors and sublimity of sublimities, she had even had it made. Anyway, she looked very remarkable in it, and I suddenly remembered Simone's letter about her in Santa Maria, looking stoic and stony. She didn't look stoic and stony now, particularly, but she did have rather an architectural look, as she had made herself up to look very pale, paler even than she is by nature, with thick grey eyebrows, rather like a sculpture, in fact. Except for one disastrous error: she had made her lips up in bright, clear scarlet. I could see the temptation, of course: after achieving the neutral, colourless harmony of skin and pale dress and dark hair the temptation to do something violent with one's mouth must have been overwhelming. But Louise's mouth isn't her best feature: it's very good, but it hasn't quite got the mobile sort of generosity to look good in that colour: it is, if anything, just a little inflexible and even censorious. Her eyes are what make her impressively, classically beautiful: she should have let them win and brood over the whole effect, by wearing no lipstick at all. In fact she looked unexpected and slightly disappointing in exactly the same way that that bust of Nefertiti did the first time I saw a picture of it reproduced in colour. And they say the Greek statues were all painted too.

Perhaps I have made too much of a point of it. She looked very beautiful and very striking in an obvious, head-turning way. That was really all there was to it. The lipstick made her look provocative as well, instead of merely aesthetic, and that was why she wore it. It must have upset Stephen.

Having thus taken her in, I could not say less than 'Well, Loulou, you're looking very beautiful.'

'Am I?' she said. 'You look very pretty yourself. You've got your hair different.'

'Not very. It's only up, not down.' At this point I noticed Stephen swimming up in the background, so I turned to greet him. He took my hand and shook it, which seemed a curious thing to do. 'Hello, Sarah,' he said, 'come along in and take your things off, you mustn't let Louise keep you standing about here in the hall.'

'Find her a drink,' said Louise, as the doorbell rang again: as I was led off to the bedroom I saw her greeting the next arrivals with an effusive embrace and 'Darling Zoë, darling Harold, how enchanting to see you, how very kind of you to come.' She sounded happy. At least she hadn't tried to kiss me. As Stephen and I progressed towards the bedroom, I was struck by the extreme newness and beauty of all the furnishings: 'What a marvellous flat,' I said, and he said, 'It is nice, isn't it? Haven't you been here before?' I didn't reply, and he left me in a big double bedroom, with instructions about how to get to the drawing-room: 'When you arrive,' he said, 'come and find me and collect a drink.' It sounded as though he expected me to take at least half an hour doing my hair, which I hardly felt to be necessary. There was another woman in the bedroom, busy powdering her nose: we smiled at each other tentatively, and I started to take off my coat. She was about thirty, and dressed in black, which made her look sophisticated, not sallow at all. The things round her neck were probably diamonds. She looked terrifying, but dull. Mentally I congratulated Louise. If one has money to spend, one might as well spend it with courage.

My coat looked extraordinarily shabby, lying on the big double bed amongst everyone else's furs, pale knitted coats, theatre evening coats, and so forth. It wasn't a bad coat in itself either, and I detest furs: it was annoying to see it made look old, in the same way that even the most hideous new shoes in shoe-shops can make one's whole outfit look decayed. The bedroom was rather impressive: when the woman in black had departed, with another non-committal smile, I felt free to look round. It was a big, high room, with a white plaster frieze and cupids on the ceiling, and it was all decorated in stone, terracotta, and pale egg blue. In front of the wide, lavishly curtained windows stood Louise's dressing-table and on it were all sorts of strange and expensive-looking glass bottles and jars. There was nothing in cut-glass. Everything was modern and faintly Scandinavian. It didn't look a bit like Louise's taste at all – not that Louise would have gone in for cut-glass powder bowls and enamel-backed brushes herself, but I didn't think she would have chosen these strange, artistic objects either. There was a brush, mirror and comb with the backs done in a most extraordinary kind of heavy pottery. I remembered Louise's dressing-table at home, littered with spilt powder, old orange-sticks, hairpins, cigarette ends, countless jars and bottles bearing the proud trade names of Rubinstein, Arden, Lancôme, Max Factor and so forth. She had never been tidy behind the scenes, as it were, but only for show. Even allowing for the fact that she had made a great effort to tidy everything away for the party, the situation looked radically changed. Presumably all the lovely bourgeois cosmetics had disappeared into these discreet, nameless glass jars – or perhaps she had risen to heights where the things one puts on one's face don't have names. I don't suppose such heights exist, but it seems incongruous and comic to picture queens and film stars and high sophisticates wearing make-up out of shops. Perhaps it was all Stephen's doing. I couldn't picture him sleeping happily in a room with a dressing-table that looked like a counter out of John Lewis's. I couldn't in fact picture him sleeping in a room with Louise at all, who had plenty of off-moments, no matter how statuesque an impression she could produce for occasions.

Suddenly I felt rather guilty and inquisitive, sitting there in their bedroom and speculating on what they looked like in bed, as if I had been reading a diary instead of simply receiving unrejectable impressions, so I hurried to reinsert a few hairpins, picked up my bag, and made my way back towards the drawing-room. It seemed full of people, but not noisily full: I saw Stephen standing by a table full of bottles and went across to him to claim my drink. Usually I drink whisky if there is any, but for some reason it seemed inappropriate so I had a gin and vermouth instead. I was surprised that all the drinks weren't in decanters: perhaps even they hadn't enough. Stephen and I exchanged a few idle remarks about Paris. He seemed rather harassed; his thin grey face was thinner and greyer than ever. After remarking that the French novel hadn't got over the basic deadlock of philosophic inversion (I think) he abruptly broke off, without even finishing his sentence, and said, 'Come on, I promised to introduce you to my old friend Wilfred Smee, he's very interested in modern youth.' I couldn't work out whether he was so imbecilic as to think I was representative of modern youth, and, thinking it, to tell me so, or whether he was simply offering the subject as a talking-point, but I followed meekly in his wake without bothering to say that I had met this man already. Stephen leads me completely out of my depth: either he never, never says anything he remotely means, or else he is really stupid, and his novels are some weird trick of fate, like medium-istic writing. I can't begin to get a grasp on him: I can't picture what he thinks or does when he's by himself: I can't even remember what he says. Somehow the décor of the house, if he really was responsible for it and not Louise, seemed to reveal more about him than anything I had ever seen him do.

He introduced me to Wilfred Smee, and we said we had met before, and he said oh had we: also to the girl Wilfred was talking to when I arrived, whom I had seen on the stage recently in a celebrated primitive drama which had managed to hit the headlines. She had been extremely good, and I told her I had enjoyed it, which pleased her: to my disappointment she seemed a very silly girl, and the oddest thing of all was that she looked exactly like what the character she had played would have looked like had she come into some money. She was wearing a tight purple dress with big bows on the shoulders, very high heels, and one of those little bits of black veil on her head with an enormous purple velvet rose stuck in the middle of it. Her stockings were black fishnet. The whole effect was very bizarre, and somehow I was delighted to see her looking like that amongst all those other subtle women, in that subtle Greek décor. She looked ghastly, but I preferred her ghastliness to everything else I felt around me. When she drifted off and the conversation seemed to flag, I asked Mr Smee if Stephen had worked out the decorations for himself: 'Oh, yes,' he said, 'he's rather good at colours and surfaces. Do you like it?'

'Very much, aesthetically,' I said.

'What do you mean by that?'

'It's just that I don't know if I'd like to live in it.'

'Ah,' he said, 'you believe in the separation of art and life.'

'I don't think so.'

'Don't you want to live in beautiful surroundings?'

'Yes, very much. Somewhere like Italy, for example.'

'Then why do you object to someone trying to make their home look beautiful? You agree that it is beautiful?'

'Oh, yes! It looks like Greek vases and things.'

'How very discerning of you,' he said, and he was sending me up, which I liked. 'As you say, it looks like Greek vases. Perhaps you only like them in museums?'

'Yes,' I said, 'I think I do. Or else in Greece.'

'It's very narrow-minded of you to want to banish a whole colour-scheme merely on account of its antiquity.'

'But everything's so new here. There aren't any antiques at all.'

'You would like a few *objets d'art*?'

'Yes. Distinctly. Yes, that's just what I've been missing. It's silly to have all this money and not to buy any objects.'

'But once you start on objects, you have to buy them all in the same period, or you end up with an artistic and historical mess.'

'Oh, a historical mess wouldn't worry me.'

'It would worry Stephen. He looks everything up in books. You couldn't put anything in this except a Grecian urn.'

'Is the whole flat the same?'

'Everywhere.'

'Even the kitchen?'

'I believe so.'

'And everything's new?'

'Again, I believe so. I can't see why you should object to its being new, if you also object to its antiquity. I thought you were a modern girl, I thought you would approve of patronizing contemporary curtain materials instead of ancient brocades.'

'That's just it. Contemporary curtains for contemporary colour schemes. Greek pots for Greek colour schemes.'

'But don't you think your sister has rather the right style for it all?'

'Classic, you mean?'

'Well, roughly speaking.'

I looked round for Louise, and saw her talking to a group of people amongst whom I located John Connell. She did in fact go very well with the decorations, though she would have gone even better if she hadn't put on the lipstick: suddenly, I was glad that she had. Her dress looked rather like a toga. I was appalled at the notion that she had bought it to go with the curtains.

'She has the style at the moment,' I said. 'But she's very variable.'

'Is she? I hadn't noticed that she was variable.'

'Perhaps she's not, any more. She used to be.' I felt, strangely enough, the impulse to defend her, which I don't remember ever having felt before, having been too busy defending myself for the past few years.

'I would have thought,' said Wilfred Smee, 'that she was invariable. Inconstant, but invariable.'

This, of course, was the most fascinating remark I had heard for weeks. My whole attention was abruptly engaged, and I had the feeling that he was about to say something of immense significance, which would reveal a whole new order of things: I waited for him, but he said nothing more, so I said, 'What do you mean, what do you mean by that?'

He looked at me and said, 'I'll tell you sometime.'

'Tell me now.'

'No. Not now. Not here.'

'Tell me. You can't make remarks like that and then not tell me.'

'I will tell you sometime, Sarah.'

His use of my christian name shut me up. I felt suspicious, as though he were about to make a pass at me, though I realized a moment later that perhaps it only meant that he didn't think of me generically, as a little sister, as Louise and John and Stephen surely did. It was conceivable that he did think of me as a human being, as he was used to my type and age, being a don. I also noticed, to my surprise, that he was rather tight. I wasn't myself, despite the ferocity of the cocktails.

I understood his reluctance to discuss Louise, for a moment later Stephen arrived, carrying a jug. A grey Finnish jug.

'How are you getting on?' he said to Wilfred, with something like bonhomie.

'Fine, fine. Talking to your wife's sister. As you told me to.'

'She's a clever little girl, isn't she?' said Stephen, as though I wasn't there. I knew this was only a conversational affectation, but it succeeded in annoying me.

'I'm only three years younger than Louise, you know,' I said.

'And how many inches shorter?'

'About three, I suppose.'

'Interesting. Interesting. Well, well. Tell me, Sarah, what do you think of Wilfred? What marks would you give him for intellect?'

'I've no idea,' I said. I don't want to make Stephen sound a total fool, but that really is the way he talks.

'He's clever too,' said Stephen. 'He knows everything there is to know about the rise of the Liberal Party in the eighteenth century.'

'Does he really?'

'Oh, everything.'

Perhaps Stephen talks like that because he is shy. Certainly he is a dead loss socially. And yet he seems to get on with people quite well. Everything he ever says, as distinct from writes, is always lacking in subtlety. He has a few ploys, a few classifications, and that is that. And yet I know he is neither stupid nor unsubtle. How or why can a person appear so little to be what they are? I cannot understand it: how should I, when my every instinct is for self-revelation, my every desire to strip myself and spill myself before the eyes of others?

I chatted a few moments more to Wilfred and Stephen, trying to be witty and unsubtle about the Liberal Party, and then Stephen removed me to talk to two television scriptwriters. He introduced me to those two with the words, 'This is my clever young sister-in-law, just down from Oxford. I'm sure she writes plays herself in her spare time.'

It made the going easy, oddly enough. Perhaps crudeness has its points, at least with the crude. I was well through my second gin by now.

Nothing of note happened for the rest of the evening really. Stephen and Louise never appeared to speak to each other once. I had a mild conversation with John about his contract and Stephen's proposed film, which apparently wasn't at all settled, owing to legal muddles: as soon as I had been talking to him for more than two minutes Louise appeared on the scene with a predatory, possessive look that was hard to mistake, though I managed, almost, to mistake it. I noticed that along one wall of the room was a bookshelf full of Louise's books: a complete set of Henry James, Lawrence Durrell, Baudelaire, an enormous new arty book called *The Face of Cleopatra* and full of paintings of same, and a complete set of Stephen's novels. This last I thought a great error of taste. I was rather preoccupied with errors of taste all evening, but I don't think it was my fault, I think it was the fault of the atmosphere generated by the furniture and the people and the hair-styles of the women. I ended up totally unenvious of Louise's new ménage, and somehow strangely sympathetic towards her. I didn't know why, as it was Stephen that looked harassed. But I felt that it was she that was suffering. I don't know why, but it was only then that I began to realize she was vulnerable. It seemed at the time like a clever and perceptive discovery, but I suppose that in fact it was extremely belated.

I don't seem to be able to describe how that party was at all. It ought to be easy, because everything is very distinct in my mind: I can visualize most of the clothes that the women wore, and how they had their hair, and that kind of thing. I can remember how people talked, in a way, and I could tell who was successful and who wasn't and who was intelligent and who wasn't. But there was something in the air that eluded me. It was almost like being in a foreign country, where distinctions are in one sense much clearer and brighter, and yet in another sense strange and very hard to assess. I think that the something in the air was a certain sort of worldliness to which I was unaccustomed and uninitiated, even though I had known for some time of its existence. Put more simply, I was socially out of my depth. I have just re-read, while thinking about this problem, one of Stephen's descriptions of a function of this kind, and I find it very hard to know precisely why I would be incapable of writing one like it. I feel it ought to be easy to sit down and write a Stephenesque account of his ménage and friends, but it isn't. It isn't really a question of observation. In the passage of Stephen that I have just been looking at there is a description of a left-wing, Bohemian, sexy-type girl, familiar enough in style and intention – the girl is made to seem very immature, very self-deluding, and so on. Yet he doesn't actually say anything about her thought processes: the whole thing is implied from various observations about her badly cut hair, the fit of her skirt over her hips, the nicotine on her fingers, and the somewhat crass, provocative things that he makes her say. The point is that I could observe these things but I could never achieve the tone or the conclusions. I could write up the actress with the purple velvet rose in these terms, but I could never feel I'd got her down on paper when I'd done it. There are hundreds of things I could say about Stephen himself – the way he holds a bottle when he is pouring out of it, very gently and yet at the same time clumsily, with no sense of shape, the way he sways slightly when he talks, the way his eyes select a spot just to the side of one's eyes when he talks to one, so that he gives the impression of contact without risking it – but they don't seem to add up to anything. They don't imply the truth.

Satire won't do. Worldliness won't do. But until you can do them both you can't do anything. Immaturity is no good, and they made me feel immature, all those people, even those I could see through: they caught undertones I couldn't, though they didn't even know they were doing it. The thing is that I couldn't start to feel them in my terms because I couldn't really feel them in theirs, and one needs the double background. Perhaps it can be learned by long apprenticeship and dedicated exploration: I hope so. Perhaps nobody is born with it. Perhaps it is only me that takes refuge in things like chance, unchartered encounters, cars in the night, roads going anywhere so long as it's not somewhere that other people know better. You can't judge or despise or even really get at something that you don't know and haven't thoroughly got, because of the fear of despising it because it's not yours. The sour grapes principle, in fact. It applies to everything. Only when one has got everything in this life, when one is eaten up with physical joy and the extreme, extending marvel of existing, can one trust oneself on the subject of the soul.

I didn't stay very long. I had a brief interchange with

Louise before I left: I sought her out to thank her for the lovely party, *etcetera*, and instead of letting me make a quick exit as I had expected she would, she seemed suddenly inclined to launch into family matters. She asked me when I had last seen our mother, and I said not since late September, when she had come up to London for some meeting or other, and to buy a new coat.

'What sort of coat?' said Louise, at once, with surprisingly normal curiosity. It was exactly the question that I would have asked.

'Oh, a kind of black curly one. Persian lamb, I think it's called. Really rather nice, as furs go.'

'Sounds rather a good idea. I hope she won't fill it too full of mothballs. Do you remember how that other one she had used to smell on speech days and things. I used to be terrified to go near her.'

'I used to think she looked marvellous in it, I don't know why – I must have been very susceptible to her opinions because I don't remember noticing that I didn't like things till I was about thirteen.'

'But she used to get such horrid things for us. Or they seemed horrid. Do you remember that olive-green pinafore dress we had? I think it got handed on to you – rather the same colour as that dress you're wearing now – I used to hate it so violently that once when she made me go out to tea in it I took another dress in a paper bag and changed in the loo. Looking back, it must have been one of the nicest things we had. It's a lovely colour.'

'I used to hate it too. Wasn't it a hand-on from Daphne?'

'That would explain it. Perhaps it was.'

'I met Daphne a week or two ago in the Tate.'

'What on earth was she doing there?'

'She'd come up for a conference.'

'Her as well. What a socially committed family we are. I believe you've even got a job?'

'Sort of. We can't all marry millionaires.'

'We can have a damn good try. Shall I introduce you to one?'

'Do you know any?'

'I don't think I do. But I know quite a lot of people who would do.'

'No thank you. Really. I'd rather wait for Francis.'

'Isn't it very awful, waiting for Francis? Or do you get around?'

'Oh, I get around. It isn't quite a question of *un seul être me manque et tout est dépeuplé.*'

'It never is, is it? The world seems quite heavily populated whatever happens. It cheers me up sometimes, to think of that.'

'Yes. It cheers me too. I say, Loulou, have you got a fur coat?'

'For goodness' sake, I'm not fifty yet, you know. Also we're not millionaires ourselves, all this décor cost a pretty penny, and then making films and so forth, it seems to spend itself somehow ... I *have* got rather a miraculous leather coat, though. Would you like to come and have a look at it? I've been dying to show it to someone. I haven't dared to wear it yet, I can't think where to go in it first – I got it in Paris. Could you bear to come and have a look?'

'I'd love to, if you don't mind leaving all your guests ...'

'Oh, they're all right, he can deal with them. Come on, you can put your things on while we're there.'

So we left the drawing-room and went off to the bedroom, which was empty, brightly lit, and piled with other people's clothes. 'It looks rather nice like this,' said Louise, 'sort of encamped and temporary.'

Strangely, I didn't feel it was her house at all, I felt as though odd circumstances had drawn us together in a hotel bedroom. There was no air of permanence in the room. She flung open one of the wardrobe doors, and I realized that what it really looked like was a film set. It was tidy and new inside the wardrobe as well as out. She searched through the row of beautiful-looking garments and eventually lit on what she was looking for: 'Look,' she said, drawing it out with a kind of comic reverence, 'Look at that, isn't it heaven, isn't it worth waiting for, isn't it the most perfect garment you ever saw in your whole life? I went in to buy a pair of shoes and I came out with this, this in a paper carrier just like a pair of pants from Marks, isn't it a joke? The shop-ladies said when I tried it on, "*Formidable, Madame.*" I've never been so utterly enraptured, so vain in my life, I walked around for the rest of the day in a coma thinking about it . . . '

'Put it on for me,' I said, 'please put it on.'

She unbuttoned it to try it on for me with a real glittering elation; I wondered if she had been drinking, or whether it really was the coat, or whether she was simply in a mood. When she had got it on she did look superb; it was a lovely thing, in very dark brown, and the leather looked soft and alive like skin. But the most extraordinary thing was her glitter, which was almost feverish; it was years since I had seen her behave so spontaneously and vividly before me, with no trace of distance or wariness. Anyone watching us would have seen a normal sisterly scene of clothes gossip and giggles in the bedroom, with no more than a trace of deliberate I'm-older-and-smarter-than-you provocation on her part. I couldn't understand why she had chosen me to show it to, unless she thought I would die of envy, and that wasn't implied in her manner at all. 'It's perfect,' I said. 'You look absolutely perfect.' She gave a little shake as I spoke and stopped looking at herself raptly in the mirror; she turned round to me quickly and said, 'It is, isn't it?' Then she gave a curious hop and a skip as though she was about to start dancing, broke off abruptly, stood absolutely still for a minute while her face composed itself into its usual classic composition, and started to undo the buttons down the front. She put it back on the hanger in silence, and I, sensing that the little game was over, turned away to unearth my own coat from the pile on the bed. When I turned back to her she was staring at herself again in the mirror, unsmiling, gravely, as though she were some object foreign to herself. I didn't interrupt, but put my things on in the prolonged silence; when I was ready to go she said, 'Well, I'd better go back to all the rest in there. Will you be able to get back all right?'

'Yes, of course,' I said. 'It isn't far to the Tube, is it?'

'No,' she said. 'It isn't far. Second on the right, first on the left.'

'All right,' I said. 'I'd better go. Will you thank Stephen for me?'

'Yes, I'll thank Stephen for you.' She held open the bedroom door and we went out and walked slowly along the hall. At the front door she said, 'Why don't you come and see me sometime?'

'I'd love to,' I said.

'I'll give you a ring some day,' she said.

'All right,' I said.

'I'll be seeing you then.'

'Yes. Thank you for the party.'

'I'm glad you came.'

'I'm glad I came too.'

'It's frightfully hot in here, isn't it? I envy you, going out. Perhaps I'll go and switch the central heating off.'

'That sounds a good idea,' I said.

'Good-bye. Remember me to Francis.'

'Good-bye.'

She shut the door behind me and I stood out there on the landing and breathed in a deep breath of relief. It had been stifling in the flat, smoky and airless, though I hadn't noticed it until she had said so. I went slowly down the stairs and through the front door where the coldness met me like another element, like the unexpected touch of cool water. I undid the top button of my coat and let the air in on my neck. Then I took off my shoes and my sore feet drank in the smooth-grained surface of the step. I took a step or two forward, a shoe in either hand, and when I was down to the pavement I began to run through all the grand spaciousness and calm of the street, as though chains had been loosed from my ankles, as though a burden had been lifted from my back.

I put my shoes on again to go down the Tube, and was just buying my ticket when I heard someone approaching me from behind, somewhat out of breath. I looked round and it was Wilfred Smee: he too had been running.

'I only just caught you,' he said. 'You run frightfully fast.'

'I do, don't I?' I said, faintly embarrassed that he had overlooked my barefoot exhibition.

'I wanted to talk to you,' he said. 'Have you eaten yet this evening? Perhaps we could go and have a meal somewhere?'

'All right,' I said. I thought I didn't like him, but I wasn't sure, and I was hungry and wanted to hear what he had to say about Louise.

'We'll eat round here, shall we?' he said, and started to direct me out of the Tube station. He walked very quickly: I had to do a kind of jog-trot to keep up with him.

'I saw you leaving,' he said, 'so I decided to come after you. Did you enjoy the party?'

'In a way,' I said. 'It was interesting.'

He laughed. 'But not amusing?'

'Oh well, it wasn't my kind of party, that's all.'

'What is your kind of party?'

'Oh, the David Vesey kind that I met you at last, I suppose.'

'The drink wasn't as nice. One thing that one can say

for Stephen, he always provides enough of the right kind of thing. Whatever criticisms one might make of the company.'

I was strongly reminded of something Louise had once said, but couldn't at the time remember it.

'What criticisms would you make of the company?' I asked, suspecting that he had probably had a lot more of the drink than I had, to be talking to me so gaily.

'Oh, they were a lot of bores, didn't you think? Not really what you might call a brilliantly intelligent gathering.'

'I don't know,' I said. 'They were most of them so much older than me that I couldn't tell.'

He laughed again. 'You mean you can only tell when people are dim if they're your own age?'

'Oh, not exactly that. Anyway, it isn't intelligence that matters at parties, is it?'

'What is it then? It is to me.'

'I like people to be amusing.'

'You like a good laugh?'

'That's right.'

'How odd. I'd have thought you were just the type for intense chats about films or books or so forth.'

'Would you? I suppose I am, but nobody ever gets quite intense enough for me. Sometimes I suspect that I must be so bloody brilliant that everybody else inevitably seems to be at half pressure. Isn't that a terrible thing to say? But you know what I mean, and that's why I gave up looking for Dostoyevskys in corners. Now I prefer a good laugh.'

'Perhaps you're not as unlike your sister as you look,' he said, but I couldn't take him up on that as we had just arrived at our goal, which was a reasonable-looking restaurant called La Calabria. When we were settled in and waiting for the *minestrone*, he said, 'I suppose you really are the clever one. Stephen's always going on about how clever you are. He admires that kind of thing.'

'Oh, Louise is clever too,' I said. 'But she did the wrong subject.'

'PPE, I believe?'

'Yes.'

'Why?'

'I can't imagine. Perversity? A passing fit of seriousness?'

'You got a first, however?'

'Certainly.'

'Therefore, the clever one.'

'Not at all. Louise would certainly have got a first too if she'd read the right subject. She got a very good second as it is, which is pretty remarkable on the amount of work she did.'

'Indeed. Indeed.' He smiled. 'I hadn't pictured such solidarity.'

'You picture us tooth and nail?'

'I'm sure that I picture you correctly.'

'The clever one and the pretty one?'

I said that to embarrass him, but I didn't succeed.

'Only a blind man could make that mistake,' he said, urbanely and literately, if not pedantically. I warmed to him. How could I help it?

'I have always tried,' I said, 'not to be like Louise. Or at least from the age of ten onwards.'

'You don't admire your sister?'

'I used to. Until I was ten.'

'I see.'

'Have you any brothers and sisters?'

'No, I was an only child.'

'How very simple for you.'

'Not if you knew my parents.'

'Do you know anyone who likes their parents?'

'No. Do you?'

'One or two. Not as many as I'd like to. Do you think

it's a tragic fact of life or a tragic fact of the English middle classes?'

'I'd never thought of it in that light. Do you think it matters?'

'Oh, desperately. I mean, it affects everything. Whether marriage means anything, and whether one ought to have children, and all sorts of practical things like that. Think how awful, to have a baby that didn't like you.'

'Are marriage and babies practical questions for you?'

'You mean, am I considering them?'

'That is more or less what I mean.'

'Well, as a matter of fact I'm more than considering it. I'm definitely going to get married when my fiancé gets back from Harvard.'

'An academic?'

'Yes, but not your line of country. Or mine. He's a historian.'

'So you're going to be a don's wife?'

'No. I'm going to marry a don.'

'And what will you be?'

'How should I know? I will be what I become, I suppose.'

'You don't find that a problem?'

How could I tell him that it was the one thing that kept me strung together in occasionally ecstatic, occasionally panic-stricken effort, day and night, year in, year out? I was on such dubious ground already, what with asserting flat out like that that I was going to marry Francis, that one lie more or less didn't matter, and I bravely made it.

'Oh,' I said grandly, 'It's no problem at all. It just happens. What happens to one, and what one does, one becomes. It's simple.'

'It sounds simple, I agree. And what about Louise? Is she, do you think, a novelist's wife?'

I thought for a moment, and then I said, 'I'm rather afraid that, oddly enough, that's all she is.'

At this point the soup arrived, and we were momentarily distracted by the Parmesan cheese and the desire to eat. I was beginning to realize that I was slightly tighter than I had thought: I was feeling very gossipy, clear-headed and garrulous, and hoped I wasn't going to say anything I would regret.

Several minutes later, during which I tried to deal discreetly with subjects like poetry, I couldn't resist attacking the flag that he had so much earlier held out.

'And what did you mean,' I said, 'by calling my sister inconstant but invariable?'

'I wondered when you would get back to that,' he said. 'My words must have struck deep for you to have remembered them so accurately.'

'I suppose they must have done. Though I really don't know what you meant by them.'

'Don't you? Surely it must have occurred to somebody of your intelligence that your sister is hardly the most faithful of wives?'

'As a matter of fact,' I said, bending my eyes intently on my plate, 'as a matter of fact it hadn't.' I think I was blushing.

'Oh surely,' said Wilfred Smee, 'my suggestion hasn't taken you by surprise. I mean a girl like your sister and a man like Stephen, surely the consequences . . . '

'The consequences?'

'I see,' he said, rather gently, 'that I have taken you by surprise. Would you rather not go on talking about this? It's entirely up to you.'

'Oh please go on,' I said. 'You can't stop now.'

'I really thought you must have been over all this in your mind as often as I have . . . '

'Oh,' I said. 'I've been over a lot of things in my mind. But I hadn't quite got to that.'

'Then where, may I ask, had you got?'

'Oh, just to the general oddness of the whole thing. I

mean, Louise and a man like that . . . But I'd better be careful. He's a friend of yours, isn't he?'

'His being a friend of mine doesn't prevent him from being, as you put it, a man like that.'

'But evidently you must think of Louise as the tiresome factor. Don't you?'

'In a way. I don't know her at all, whereas I know Stephen quite well. And while it seems to me to be perfectly evident why Stephen married her, I can't for the life of me imagine why she married *him* – especially in view of the way that she apparently intends to lead her married life.'

'Please tell me what, precisely, you mean by that.'

'I mean, I suppose, that she is at the moment, and has been since, I believe, before the wedding, very blatantly having an affair with John.'

'John Connell?'

I must have known it because the information didn't come in any way as a surprise, but rather as a confirmation of everything I had expected. Nevertheless, it took my breath away, to hear it stated like that. He simply nodded to my query, and all I could say was:

'How odd. How very odd. I might have known it.'

'It is odd, isn't it? I mean, there was no need at all for her to marry Stephen. She could probably have married John if she had wanted to. It all seems unnecessarily tortuous.'

'When you say blatantly, do you mean that everyone knows but me?'

'A lot of people do know. She certainly makes no attempt to conceal it. In fact, she seems to display it to the world at large, as though she enjoyed the situation . . . '

That rang a bell. 'I'm sure,' I said quickly, 'that she does. It's the sort of thing she would enjoy. She likes drama.'

'That, of course, is one of the possible explanations.'

'But one would hardly marry to enjoy having an affair with someone else.'

'It does sound a little far-fetched, I agree.'

'Not too far-fetched, though.'

'Well, you would know.'

I raised my eyebrows at that. 'About her, I mean,' he explained. 'That's all I implied!'

'No,' I repeated, 'it really isn't too far-fetched.'

'She's always been like this?'

'Like what?'

'Keen on provocation.'

'Oh, madly. She's one of those that enjoy it more than the real thing.'

'The real thing?'

'Love. That was what I meant. Love.'

'Oh yes.'

'When you say that a lot of people know, does that include Stephen?'

'Oh, I think so. I don't know how long he's known, but he certainly knows by now.'

'And what does he think about it?'

Wilfred smiled, a tolerant smile, which made me feel childish, but which also betrayed a deeper anxiety than I had yet suspected in him.

'Naturally,' he said, 'he is more than a little disturbed. I don't think anyone enjoys having their wife commit adultery with their closest friend.'

'That word sends a real Old Testament chill through me,' I said.

'What? Adultery?'

'Don't say it. It sounds awful.'

'Well, to some people it is. To Stephen, for example. It offends his high church leanings.'

'I didn't know he had any. How can he have, and write books like that?'

'Why not?'

'Oh well,' I said, as nastily as I could, 'I suppose you can say this for Anglicanism, that at least it's rich and respectable. I can't see Stephen believing in anything ridiculous, like God. He chooses to believe in something good, solid and social, like the sacrament of marriage instead.'

Wilfred must have noticed that it wasn't really in my nature to be rude about other people's friends, because he said, 'I'm sorry, Sarah, I can see I've upset you.'

'Oh, that's all right,' I said. 'I think I've been hatching this bit of awareness for months. I've probably known it since their wedding-day. It has upset me, I admit it's upset me, but I can't think why, as I don't think I care very much for Louise, and I don't think I care very much about marriage, in the abstract. I can't think why I mind so much. Perhaps it's just a hangover from those days before I was ten. When everything she did affected me. Because I knew I'd have to do it too, one day. When my family were a part of me.'

'You're sure they're not now?'

'Well, the shock of this is almost enough to make me wonder. It is amazing, I get taken by surprise by myself in the most extraordinary ways . . . Who would have thought that an emancipated girl like me should actually feel concerned about a trivial thing like this? I almost feel it my duty not to feel concerned.'

'Why on earth?'

'Oh, for so many reasons. For so many principles, really. The principle of non-interference. The principle of not caring twopence about anything Louise ever says or does again. The principle of marriage not binding those who don't want to be bound. And so on.'

'But in practice, to use your own word, you are shocked?'

'I suppose that must be it. My stupid cowardly little

super ego at it again. If I don't tame that nasty creature soon it will get the better of me. In fact, you know, I admire Louise for having bashed hers up so successfully. She doesn't seem to hear any little whispers from the past ages of morality during the long night watches.'

'Are you sure of that? You think her conduct leaves her completely without qualms?'

I hesitated, and thus significantly belied my own response.

'Oh, I'm quite sure. I'm sure Louise is quite above such pettiness.'

'All magnificent ego?'

'That's right.'

'It's an odd ideal.'

'Is it? That's what I would like to be. If I understand the terms correctly, not having read Freud. But tell me, you said just now that you knew why Stephen had married Louise. Do tell me, because it's always puzzled me . . . I should have thought he simply wasn't the marrying type. In fact, since I've exposed so many nïavetés to you already, I might as well go the whole way and tell you that at one time I seriously wondered if he weren't queer. I think that's what anyone would guess, from reading his books. Their funny social bitchiness, if you know what I mean.'

'Yes, I do know what you mean.'

'Tell me why he married her.'

'I think because he loved her. He's always been attracted by her peculiar brand of – how shall I put it – her peculiar desperateness. She's not, in any sense, a frivolous person. Of course, she has all the obvious qualities that Stephen wouldn't marry without – beauty, popularity, even notoriety – and then on top of it all she has this intenseness. She overdoes all her emotions. Or seems to. Stephen's always been attracted by girls of that type – at Cambridge there was a succession of them, high-powered, pretty girls, the daughters of earls and artists, all despising life and themselves and fanatically in pursuit of happiness . . . you get the picture?'

'What happened to them all?' I asked, and as I asked I had a flash of intuition, and answered my own question. 'I know what happened to them,' I said. 'They all met very highly-sexed men and fell in love and got reconciled to life and got married. Right?'

'Absolutely right.'

'And the problem in this instance is, why did Louise marry Stephen instead of the requisite highly-sexed man John?'

'The problem is complicated by the fact that John had already abducted one of these girls, years ago. Perhaps you've heard of her. She calls herself Sappho Hinchcliffe.'

'The actress?'

'That's right.'

'What was she like?'

'Oh, she was a highly intelligent girl, one of the best. I was in love with her myself. She and Stephen had a kind of morbid affection for each other . . . John always said that she felt all the emotions that Stephen was incapable of, and wh ch he wanted to write about. A sort of extended aesthetic insight. And then John became interested, and Sappho couldn't resist him, and there was a lot of heart-ache right through Tripos. She and Stephen had desks immediately next to each other for nearly all the papers, and she would sit there crying and chewing her pen, and would walk out an hour early from each to go on the river with John . . . oh, what a life. It was all very romantic. I suppose it all still sounds reasonable to you, instead of absurd. I must be getting old. I can't think of it as any-thing but absurd.'

'I can see it all,' I said. And I was thinking, but for Francis, there went I.

'But she didn't marry either of them.'

'Oh no. She had a career instead. Not a very steady one, but distinguished. I see her from time to time. So does Stephen.'

'Is she happy?'

'Yes. Very.'

'And you three have remained friends through all this to-do?'

'Oh yes.'

'That sounds a little sick to me.'

'Sick?'

'Unhealthy.'

'Perhaps it was. Civilized behaviour is sick isn't it?'

'Is that intended to reprove me?'

'Not really. I must confess that even I felt at times that it would be a lot better if somebody hit somebody. And now, in this present situation. I am very much concerned that somebody will.'

'Stephen?'

'No, I was thinking that Stephen might get hit.'

'Oh dear. And what will happen to Louise?'

'If she's not careful she may well get herself into a first-class scandal.'

'Oh, surely not. None of them are important enough for that.'

'Well, a second-class scandal. That would be bad enough.'

'You don't think she might like it? Don't you think it might be rather the kind of thing she thrives on? Like desperation?'

'I don't think she would really like it at all. Though she might think she might, I agree. But in the end she would find it humiliating. Though really, you know, I'm not at all concerned about her – I'm concerned about Stephen. I think he does feel humiliated, and he's taken enough humiliation in his life. If anyone's sick, he is – he's what you'd call a sick man. He's not been looking at all well recently, and I'm afraid it may break out. He never talks about Louise, and he's not writing – he hasn't written a word since he met her, I don't think. His last novel came out three years ago. If you ask me, I think he's heading for some kind of collapse. You know John went over to Paris for the weekend to see them – he told me it was pathetic to see them both, Louise as bored as hell, telling other literary men how good she thought her husband's books were, and about this film, and wasn't he brilliant and promising and so forth, and Stephen doing nothing but look miserable and watch her whoever she was talking to and try to overhear what she was saying – I definitely think there's a serious danger he might collapse.'

'You really surprise me. I thought only intense people had collapses.'

'Intense people collapse, but they also survive. They feed on disaster. So did Sappho and all the other girls. But for Stephen it isn't a game. With him it isn't a question of pushing to see how far he can go. With him it might mean permanent disablement.'

'What *do* you mean?'

I was horrified by this glimpse of abysses so beyond anything I had ever imagined.

'When I said that Stephen was a sick man,' Wilfred went on, 'I didn't mean that he found life faintly tragic or mildly meaningless, or anything like that – I mean that he really is a psychological case. People use the word neurotic to describe anything they like, and forget that some people really are neurotic, and have real illnesses of the mind. And a real case isn't glamorous or intense or anything like that – he's just ill and cut off and unapproachable. That's what Stephen is like. I know him well, and I know. It isn't interesting, it's sad and boring. He's been getting worse. There used to be days when he would emerge and face what was happening to him – now he never does, never, and there's nothing his friends can do except stand around and try to stop him getting hurt. It's like looking after a chronic invalid or a baby. I'm not even interested any more, except for the sake of the past, and because someone has to be. I feel responsible. I know it's presumptuous of me to assume that I know more about it than his wife, but I feel sure that she's precisely the kind of person who would be incapable of appreciating how bad he is, that he really can't feel things normally at all . . . do you understand me?'

'Not really. Only very vaguely. If Stephen is as bad as you suggest he is, how on earth can he write books?'

'Well, his art isn't exactly of the most human kind, is it? And then, a lot sicker men than him have written a lot better books. Look at John Stuart Mill. And then again, he's not writing at the moment, which worries me more than anything – I'm convinced he used to find some kind of release in writing, a sort of substitute existence, full of emotions and humanity and so forth, and above all full of people – '

'I'm out of my depth,' I said.

'You aren't with me at all?'

'It's so completely out of my world of reference – I've never been faced with anything like this before. Do you mean he's mad?'

'You do put things bluntly, don't you, my dear. No, I don't mean precisely that . . . I do, however, mean that he's a case for a specialist, not for all our amateur guess-work. Don't you feel that there are whole areas of his personality that never come to light?'

'I always felt he was meaningless. Sort of nothing and meaningless.'

'That's one way of describing it.'

'But what is it that's wrong with him? Is it curable?'

'I don't know. I doubt it. I'm afraid he's one of those unfortunate people who are always one up on their doctors, and so beyond help – '

'But as to what it is . . . '

'My dear child, you're a silly girl. You think you're brave and can take everything, don't you? You don't like to be spared, do you? Well, I am old-fashioned enough to be able to decide that it would be better for you if I didn't go into it.'

'Perhaps I'm grateful to you. Perhaps I don't want to know.'

'I'll tell you this much. You know that all these words one uses so gaily at parties, like masochism and sadism, have real meanings, don't you? Real, factual meanings, like mumps and measles?'

'Yes, I knew that.'

'Then you see what I mean.'

'Yes, I see what you mean.'

'Then you see that I am justified in feeling concern on his behalf?'

'I suppose so. You think that Louise is going to precipitate some ghastly crisis and everything will snap.'

'In a way.'

'Will it matter?'

'Of course it will matter. Things are bad, but not as bad as they might be, by a long way.'

'Just tell me, what do you get out of it?'

'Out of what?'

'Out of all your concern?'

'Nothing. Nothing but the satisfaction of having tried. Nobody else is interested, so somebody has to be. It's not very exciting, I agree.'

'It's like being God,' I said.

He smiled. 'Yes, I sometimes feel tempted to feel that. But unlike Stephen I don't believe in God, so either I take an interest myself or consign him to the human rubbish-dump.'

'How terrible.'

'It is.'

'Is there nobody that cares but you? I thought John Connell was a friend of his too?'

'Ah yes, but their relationship is only one of mutual aid . . . this film they talk about, but will never make, rather aptly symbolizes it . . . and anyway, under the circumstances, it would take a remarkable degree of detachment, I think . . . '

'So nobody cares but you?'

He paused. 'Doesn't it strike you as odd that you, the sister of his wife, should be asking me that?'

I had to think for a moment before I realized what he meant. 'Yes. Yes, of course,' I admitted. 'Husband and wife, husband and wife. Not that I have any faith in the idea at all with those two. I suppose that it's just conceivable that on some deeper level she cares about him, but I think it's terribly unlikely. He would need someone self-sacrificing and devoted, wouldn't he? Somebody more interested in him than in herself.'

'And for that Louise wouldn't qualify?'

'Well, would she?'

'Oh, I agree. I never had any hopes of her.'

'She's a taker, not a giver.'

'Perhaps you can tell me what, in marrying him, she expected to take?'

'Now *there's* a question. I've thought about this several times, believe me. Do you know what I decided in the end? That she didn't know what else to do so she got married. It sounds too bourgeois to be true, doesn't it, just the kind of thing that all that higher education ought to have knocked out of us – but the fact is that when she came down a couple of years ago she had no idea of what to do with herself. There wasn't any career she was passionately interested in, so she just messed around for a year, in and out of people's beds I don't doubt, and then started a job in advertising. I ask you, Louise sitting in an office trying to sell things – the idea was ludicrous. And yet, what could she do? I didn't quite get this at the time because I was still up myself and overflowing with love and optimism – but since I came down I see what she was getting at. She was far too intelligent to do nothing, and yet too beautiful and sexy to do all the first-class things like politics or law or social sciences – and she was naturally afraid of subsiding into nothingness, I suppose. Or that's what I guess she felt, from what I myself am feeling. Our situations are very similar.'

'But not your ways of solving them?'

'Oh, I don't solve things. I just drift and struggle as the weeks float on.'

'But Louise thought that marrying Stephen was her way out of doing nothing?'

'I think so. After all, he is very different from all the boys in Birmingham that we might have been marrying, and he has a lot of money, and he is famous . . . or does all that mean that she just succumbed to social pressures? I suppose it does. But on her own terms, that's the point. I think she's getting her pound of flesh from society for not letting her live as what she is.'

'*Via* Stephen?'

'Yes, admittedly, *via* Stephen.'

'It's hardly very generous of her.'

'I don't think she has the objectivity to be generous. She thinks her own life is so much more interesting than anyone else's that she has a right to sacrifice others – she has a point, too I think, but I agree that she ought not to be endangering her husband's sanity, if you really think she is doing something as melodramatic as that . . . it's a pity she didn't pick someone better able to look after themselves. But it all seems so unlikely to me. I would have thought that of the two she was much more unstable.'

'Would you really? I had concluded, from I admit a much briefer acquaintance, that she was hard as nails.'

I pondered this description, and decided, 'Yes, in a way I think you're right.'

I was at this point remembering discussing normality and extremes with Stephen at his wedding: it seemed peculiarly ironic that I had then thought of myself as being more eccentric than he was.

'Does he know himself that he's in such a bad way?' I asked.

'Oh yes, I think he knows all right. Sometimes he seems to be perfectly lucid about his own state of mind, but much more often he seems to think that everyone else is like him – he must do a lot of double thinking.'

'What did he hope to get out of marrying Louise?'

'How should I know? Perhaps he hoped to catch a little of her intensity. To live off her energy. Perhaps he hoped she would understand him. Perhaps he simply wanted to get hold of her, to appear as her owner, when she'd turned down so many others. Including John. It must have looked to him at one point as though he'd beaten John.'

'What on earth do you think will happen?'

'I've no idea. Couldn't you try asking Louise what she's up to?'

'Oh God no, don't ask me to interfere, you can't imagine what bad terms Lou and I are always on, I couldn't talk straight to her to save my life.'

'No. Somehow I didn't think you would.'

'Why don't you try finding out from John?'

He laughed. 'That wouldn't be quite the same thing. Do you think she's in love with him?'

'I've really no idea.'

'I think John is quite seriously taken with her. But it won't last. He's a great one for passing passions. Being so attractive himself, he can afford to be.'

'He is attractive, isn't he?'

'Do you find him so?'

'Oh, fabulously.' The more I thought about this, the

truer it seemed. 'He's one of those people,' I said, 'that I resent because they're so obviously wonderful. You know, he just gives you a look and you start twitching.'

'Dangerous, isn't it?'

'Perhaps Louise is in love with him. Is he a serious kind of person?'

'Oh very, I suppose.'

'Because she couldn't be in love with anyone less serious than her.'

And as I said that, I realized what it was that Louise and I really had in common. We were both serious people.

There our conversation more or less ended. We both sobered up considerably over the coffee, and I at least began to wonder if I had said anything that would be likely to get reported back to its subject-matter. If I had, it was too late. And I had said worse things about Louise before. Also, Wilfred had said much more compromising things to me than I had to him.

I went home on the Tube. On the way back I kept thinking of a programme I once saw on television about schizophrenic children: strange, bright little children who lived in a severed world and did not recognize other people as people at all, and climbed over their mothers as though they were part of the furniture. They talked a private language, arranged things in neat lines, made odd little gestures with their hands, and broke their mothers' hearts, I do not doubt. I remember there was one enchanting small child called Henry, aged three, who acknowledged the existence of nobody except, for one fleeting second, when his mother violently kissed his arm: then he leaned back and shut his eyes in pleasure, like a child, like a normal living child. The psychiatrist kept insisting that the condition was rare and biochemical, but it seemed oddly metaphysical to me. Which just shows how willing one is to attach glamorous reasons to sickness, provided there is nothing to repel. In fact I suppose a

Mongol would bring more joy. He also said that an apparently similar condition could be found in small children who had been ignored by their parents, but that the neglect had to be almost total. That upset me more than anything – the thought of those sad, borderline children who clung on to sanity and childhood through the few scraps of affection and interest that accidentally fell their way. The human mind is not a delicate plant, I thought: on the contrary, it will survive almost anything, and what could have happened to Stephen to have pushed him out beyond the borderline? Do not expect an answer to that question, because there is none.

I thought over what Wilfred had said continually, without seeming to get anywhere. There seemed to be a lot of clues around, which would one day, but not yet, fit into a pattern. I didn't do anything about getting to see he myself: I didn't feel it would be appropriate to invite her round for coffee. So I waited, and as chance would have it the next news I heard of her was from a quite unexpected source – my cousin Michael, between me and whom there existed, as I have explained, a certain *rapport*. Michael is a medical student in his fourth or so year at a hospital in Oxford, and on the whole I see him only at family gatherings, though occasionally he used to look me up at college. Anyway, about a week after the party at Louise's, he rang me up and asked if he could come round to supper. I said Yes, and we had quite a pleasant meal of packet soup *etcetera*, and talked about Daphne and his latest girl-friend and when I was going to get married. He had come up, if you please, to watch a football match. Just as we were talking about a woman he had seen in the hospital who had been horribly squashed by a bus, he broke off to say, 'And, by the way, I saw your friend Martin in Paris.'

'Did you really? By what way?'

'What way?'

'I mean, why did you think of him?'

'Oh, I was thinking of those plastic bombs. I saw someone in Paris when I was with him, almost blown up. I had to go and help.'

'How awful, what happened?'

'Oh, he got taken off to hospital.'

'And how was Martin?'

'Great.. He's a nice chap, isn't he? He took me out to a nice spot or two. He sends you his love.'

'He's not thinking of coming back again?'

'I doubt it.'

'He was nice to me, Martin. Did you meet any nice girls while you were with him?'

'They all talked French. Except for one American and she was too fast for me.'

'Oh, Michael.'

'Guess who else I met there?'

'I can't.'

'Louise and Stephen.'

'Go on, you didn't.'

'Yes, I did.'

'On purpose?'

'Good Lord no! I was just wandering across by the Louvre, on my way to see Martin actually, when I saw them sitting outside a café. They asked me to go and have coffee with them.'

'Did you?'

'Well, I kind of had to.'

'What were they doing?'

'Just sitting.'

'Sitting and doing what?'

'I don't know. Talking, I suppose.'

'Was it a posh café?'

'I think it was probably a hotel.'

'What did you talk about?'

'I can't really remember. I think I asked them how long their honeymoon was going on, and Louise said it wasn't a honeymoon, it was business. So I said what business, and she said something about a film or something. Some French director wants to make a film of one of his books.'

'Oh, a *French* director. That would explain it.'

'Explain what?'

'How anyone could ever be so idiotic as to want to film a book by Stephen. Have you ever read any of his things, Michael?'

'I can't say I have, no. What are they like?'

'Oh, ghastly. Good but ghastly.' I had been increasingly realizing that Stephen's books really were good, of their arid kind. And there is a place for aridity. So let it be said here, finally, that his books are good.

'I don't think they're my kind of thing,' said Michael. 'I had a look at one once, it was all about civil servants and politicians and love affairs.'

'Aren't you interested in that kind of thing?'

'Lord no. Are you?'

'I suppose I am.'

'You always were a funny one.'

'Tell me, did you think Louise looked happy?'

'Funny you asked me that. I thought she looked pretty bored. She looked very smart, you know how she does, but she looked really fed up. I asked her if she liked Paris, and she said not very much, she thought it was too full of intellectuals and beatniks. I said I'd have thought she'd have liked that kind of thing, and she was furious with me.'

'How do you mean, furious?'

'Well, she said, "Oh shut up, Michael, don't be so silly." I remember quite clearly her saying that. She never had much sense of humour, your sister. Always taking offence.'

'Did she really say "Shut up"?'

'Oh yes.'

'Was Stephen listening?'

'Sort of. He never pays me the slightest attention, that man. He gives me the creeps. I suppose he thinks I'm not worth sucking up to.'

'Did Louise say anything else interesting?'

'Well, she asked after you.'

'Did she?'

'Yes, she asked what were you doing now. I told her you were working for the BBC, and she said she wondered how long that would last. She really is stupid whenever your name comes up, you know. Then I told her I'd been seeing this friend of yours, Martin, and about a place he'd taken me to the night before with singers and all that, you know – well, I had to say something – and she said it all sounded very undergraduate. So I asked her where they spent their time, and she was furious again, she said they weren't on holiday and they didn't go out to amuse themselves. I can't stick your sister, I'm afraid.'

'She can be terrible. She sounds as though she was very gloomy.'

'That's what I thought. I thought he probably didn't take her out enough. I bet she'd have been glad to come out with Martin and me. He's a real pain in the neck, that man.'

'Did he say anything at all?'

'Not to me. Apart from the fact that it was jolly fine weather, wasn't it?'

'Was it?'

'Not bad.'

'Did you gather what they'd just been doing or were just about to do?'

'No. They didn't seem to be doing anything.'

'Poor Louise. Not my idea of a honeymoon.'

'Well, she asked for it. If she will go mixing with characters like that, what does she expect? She gets worse and worse, she really does. She's the most affected person I've ever met.'

'Affected?'

'Well, isn't she? Always carrying on as though she's so sophisticated and knows so much more than anyone else. And as though she's so important. She acts as though her bloody husband were Charles Dickens.'

'Do you think so?'

'She's always trying to give the impression of how important he is. He's not all that important, is he? I'd never heard of him before she got engaged.'

'I suppose he is quite important, really. He's very well-known, you know, though not among illiterate medical students. Most people who read have heard of him.'

'Daphne thinks his books are shocking.'

'Did she tell you so?'

'Well, unpleasant was the word she used, but I know what she meant.'

'Poor Daphne. Do you think she'll ever get married?"

'I don't know.'

'I'd rather be like my sister than yours.'

'You are more like.'

'Do you think I'm affected, Michael?'

'Sometimes.'

'What do you think will happen to Louise?'

'I don't know. It's her funeral, isn't it?'

'Yes. Yes, it is.'

'She could always get divorced and marry somebody else, couldn't she?'

'You make it sound very easy.'

'Oh, I don't know anything about all that kind of thing.'

'I think she spends her time giving boring dinner parties for Stephen's boring literary friends. Literary people are death, I should think. They're always much nastier about each other than any other people I know are about their colleagues. I suppose she could go on giving dinner parties all her life.'

'Perhaps she'll have a baby.'

'Do you mind.' The idea outraged me. 'Honestly, can you picture her pregnant?'

He laughed. 'It happens to the most surprising people,' he said. 'You should see some of the cases I've seen.'

'Michael, did you hear all about it when Louise got engaged? Was there a terrible to-do? Why did they get married so soon after it was all fixed up? When I went away in July nobody had breathed a word, and the first I heard of it was a letter from Mama telling me about it and asking me to go home to be a bridesmaid. Loulou didn't write to me at all about it.'

'I didn't hear much about it either. I was rowing at Henley. But Daphne told me there was a great row, because your father couldn't stand Stephen. Your mother liked him, apparently, because he kept sending her flowers, but your father couldn't stand him.'

'I'm not surprised.'

'I don't know why they had such a short engagement.'

'Perhaps she was afraid of changing her mind.'

'Perhaps she wishes she had.'

'Yes, perhaps she does.'

And there we left it.

The very next day I myself had a desultory and accidental encounter with them. It was a bitterly cold day: I had just been to Bush House and was waiting at a bus stop in the Aldwych to catch a bus home. It was just after half past six, and there didn't seem to be any buses at all. My feet were getting colder and colder, and I kept wondering if I ought to go up to Holborn and catch a Tube, but hadn't the willpower to move. I had bought a copy of the *Evening Standard*, but my hands were so cold that I didn't want to take them out of my pockets to turn over the pages. I was just standing and being miserable when I heard somebody shouting at me, and when I looked around I saw that it was Louise shouting from a car window. She was in the far stream of traffic, and things were piled up and hooting behind.

'Hi, Sarah,' she shouted. 'Hi.'

'Hallo,' I yelled back.

'Come over here,' she shouted, imperiously. Everyone was staring at her, the whole bus queue and the other pedestrians and the other motorists. It took me a minute or two to get across, as the traffic on my side of the road was still moving: when I got there she leant right out of the car window and said, 'Where are you going? Come and have a drink with us.'

'I was going home,' I said. 'Where are you going?'

'We're going to the theatre,' she said, 'with these two friends here in the back.'

I peered into the back, as I could hardly help but do, and saw a somewhat oldish-looking man and his wife. They did not look an amusing couple.

'Come on,' said Louise. 'Get in the back quick. The traffic's all waiting behind.'

I got in as I was told. It was delightfully warm in the car. Stephen introduced me to the other people: they were American, and the woman was wearing a fur coat. I gathered later that they were potential backers for the potential film, which would explain Louise's odd mixture of charm and rudeness. Half the time she tried to be her very nicest, flashing dazzling smiles at them, but occasionally a streak of offhand contempt would show itself, as it had in her curious phrase 'these two friends here in the back'. Stephen, on the other hand, was purely and simply out to please. As soon as I grasped the situation, I immediately decided that Louise had picked me up in order to aggravate already existing tensions, but long afterwards she told me that although this had been her intention, it hadn't in fact worked out like that, as Stephen was rather keen on me as an image of the young bright set, and considered me a picturesque illustration of London culture. Even pink with cold and wearing an old wool hat. We went to one of those theatrical pubs behind Drury Lane. They were going to see *The Cherry Orchard* at the Aldwych: I said how lovely, and Louise in one of her most deliberately off-moments said, 'I've seen it twice already.'

She seemed to know quite a lot of people in the pub, many more than Stephen did: they kept greeting her with, 'Hallo, darling' from time to time. This didn't go down at all well with Stephen, until he noticed how well it went down with his two back-seat backers, and from then on he decided to treat the matter as an endearing joke.

'Who on earth was *that*, my sweet?' he asked, as a peculiarly queer young man patted her shoulder and said, 'Bye-bye, darling' on his exit.

'Oh, an actor,' said Louise. 'He's at the Duchess, I think.'

Stephen glanced at his couple and offered them another drink. They said No. Then he offered me one, and I thought I had better leave. I had been interested in the type of the two people, but having got as much of it as I was capable of – American, sub-intelligent, rich, would-be internationally cultured, ugly – I had become bored. I felt sorry for Louise, who had to spend the evening in their company, and was glad that I had myself no boring social obligations. The thought of having to win money or approval from others, when both themselves and me would be quite aware of what I was attempting to do, made me feel full of disgust. I have not the slightest yearning for any kind of power. I knew Louise must be as bored as I would have been. And I felt sorry for her. It seemed to be becoming almost a habit with me.

As I took my leave and thanked them for the drink, I wondered at the social meaninglessness of all our meetings. I never saw Louise except by accident or at parties. And all we ever did when we saw each other was drink the odd drink, exchange a platitude or two, and wait till the next time. And that seemed to be all there was to it. Perhaps she was neither more nor less than all the other people I was on drinking terms only with. We never met each other with any purpose or any bond. Except the wedding, of course: that had been full of some kind of purpose. But since then – and, indeed, before then – all I had ever seen or heard of her had been on the most flippant, let's have a gin and tonic level. Let's go for a drive in the car, let's have a party, let's look at my leather coat, let's go and have a drink before the show. What was so wrong with it all? What was wrong was that she, no more than me, was flippant. It would have to break down some day.

After this episode, a week or so of dreary doldrums elapsed. All the 'I love yous' with which I filled my letters to Francis, *faute de mieux*, seemed more of a gesture of faith than usual. Nothing continued to happen, except for one stirring postcard from Simone, who was apparently still in Rome: on the front there was a picture of the jewelled Bambino from Santa Maria in Ara Coeli, and on the back she had written in her spiky distinguished script, 'How do you like this baby in its jewelled sleeping-bag?' and a quotation from Byron, about O Rome, the Niobe of nations, the orphans of the heart shall turn to thee. The orphans of the heart, what a phrase: sometimes I wish I had the constancy entirely to pursue the image of my desolation. But I lack constancy to any image: I am constant only to effort.

Then, one evening, about three weeks after my chat with Wilfred, I was flicking through a copy of that notorious gossip-paper in which I had literally bought my fish and chips, when I discovered a grease-stained picture of Louise and John. I leapt to attention and read the accompanying bit of oblique slander: they had been to a charity matinée together, and the caption said, 'Mrs Stephen Halifax, wife of the novelist, with her friend John Connell. "My husband is so busy writing a film script," she said, "that he hadn't time to come." Mrs Halifax was married last September.'

I must confess that a shiver went through me at the sight of my sister in such a prominent and pilloried position: I wondered what our parents would think of it, and all the old acquaintance of our innocence. I couldn't at all work out whether I was shocked or concerned or disinterested or what: it was one of those cases where one's superficial lack of response seems almost to indicate deeper layers of impression. I didn't feel horrified, as I had no doubt that Daphne, if told what I now assumed to be the facts of the case, would be: but I felt dimly unquiet, as though some profound but obscure personal wound had been inflicted. I was sitting thinking about this and eating the last few damp chips when the telephone rang. I had a premonition that it was going to be somebody tiresome, but when I did answer, it was Louise.

'Is that you, Sal?' her voice came, thin and clear, and I knew that she wanted something. She always does when she calls me Sal.

'Yes, it's me. How are you?'

'Oh fine, fine. How are you?'

'Surviving . . . '

'Has Mama been to see you?'

'Mama? No, why, should she have been?'

'Oh, I just thought she might have been . . . She was in town, she gave me a ring last night. I thought she might have been to see you.'

'No, I didn't even know she was here. How is she?'

'How do you expect?'

'I'm surprised she didn't give me a ring . . . perhaps I was out.'

'Perhaps she just wanted to tell me off.'

'What about?'

'Oh, first of all about that silly picture of John and me in the paper . . . did you see it?'

I took a gasp at angels rushing in where I feared *etcetera* and answered, rather proud of the penurious note in my reply, 'As a matter of fact, I was just eating fish and chips out of the copy with it in. It's not a bad photo, is it? What did Mama say?'

'Oh, she said various things about it not being dignified, and this and that, you know . . . she doesn't really mind, she was tickled pink by that one in the *Tatler*. She was rather annoyed, though, about Daphne.'

'What about her, for goodness' sake?'

'Oh, it's nothing really . . . just that Daphne happened to call when she was in London doing some Christmas shopping, or something, and paying her duty visit to *My Fair Lady*, or whatever, and like an idiot I asked her round for a drink and then went and forgot all about it. I wasn't in when she called . . . talk about psychological slips of memory . . . anyway, she actually went and *told* Mama, which I thought pretty low, even by her own old school standards, so I got a little moral thingummy from Mumsy about relations, and all the rest of it . . . apparently you had gone and blackened my case by having her to tea or something with a young man, as mother put it . . . who on earth did you sacrifice?'

'Oh, it was only Lovell,' I said, remembering, 'and we all met quite by accident in the Tate. There's no lofty moral tone about that, is there?'

'Well, Mama got it all wrong, as usual, and I got it in the neck. And do you know what Mama suggested, as compensation, I suppose?'

'No?'

'She said why didn't I invite Daphne to stay for a few days next time she was in London for one of these conferences or whatever. Well, I ask you? Did you ever hear of anything so inconceivable? A visit from Daphne. I suppose that's Mummy's idea of social life, married daughters having the family to stay . . . she'll be inviting herself next, just when I thought I'd got out of all that. But honestly, Sal, did you ever hear the like. Daphne in our house. I just couldn't reply I was so dumbfounded . . . And she didn't even seem to realize the enormity of what she was saying. How can people be so obtuse?'

'Obtuse to what?'

'To the impossibility, of course.'

'To the clash, do you mean, of types?'

'Yes. that's what I mean. Daphne and Stephen under one roof. It was bad enough having her as bridesmaid, which they insisted on . . . if Stephen had been the kind of man who is capable of arguing we'd never have put up with it.'

'I must say I wondered . . . '

'You missed all that fuss, didn't you? I had to give in, I said to myself, this is the last, the very last thing, that I'm ever going to do in the name of duty . . . and then they start getting at me to have people to stay . . . it's so stupid. I mean could you do it?'

'Of course I couldn't. Not even to martyr myself . . . she depresses me so unbearably, every time I speak to her I end up feeling kind of debased and wicked and guilty . . . '

'Do you really? She doesn't make me feel wicked, she makes me feel predatory . . . after all, one can scarcely think of people like that as human beings. She's like a different species, don't you think.'

'Loulou, how horribly apt.'

'It's good, isn't it. A different species. There's really no point in pretending that she's a human being like me because she so obviously isn't. She reminds me of those tame shabby animals in zoos, odd gnus and cows and things, so docile and herbivorous that they don't even bother to put them behind bars, but let them wander around loose . . . all the boring animals. Herbivores. Sadly smelling, depressed animals. You know what I mean?'

'And you feel you're a carnivore?'

'Well, if that is the opposite of a Daphne, yes, I do. And you too. We're the predatory type, don't you think? The flesh eaters? I'd rather eat than be eaten. If Daphne weren't another species I would have to feel sorry for her, but as it is . . . ' She paused, at loss for a fanciful conclusion.

'As it is,' I said, 'you devour her unashamed.'

'Oh, I don't deliberately devour . . . '

'But one does feed off them . . . '

'If you mean that my way of life – our way of life – exists through the existence of theirs . . . well, yes, I suppose one does. It is a minority way, isn't it, Sal? Money, theatres, books . . . '

'Speak for yourself about money,' I said, and then wished I hadn't, as I feared it would close her up, but it didn't. 'No,' she went on, 'not money, but you can't pretend you're not one of the most exclusive of all . . . the most predatory . . . for all your fish and chips, SallyO, and your down-at-heel shoes . . . you know what I mean, we're in it together, you and I.'

You cannot accuse Louise of slowness.

'And we can't live without the herbivores?'

'How could we? We live by our reflection in their eyes.'

'I hope not,' I said. And I meant it, but I knew that she was terribly, intimately right. I had never, literally never, heard such words of intimacy from her before. It made a pause in the conversation as I couldn't take her up, and then she went on, 'But what I really rang you about, Sarah, was something that I wanted you to help me out with. A problem of entertaining.'

'Not entertaining Daphne. You can do your own slaughtering.'

'Oh no, not Daphne. Not as bad as that. But stiff enough, in its own way. Stephen won't be in, and I tried to get Jessica to come and leaven the lump, but she's engaged . . . '

'Come on,' I said, 'out with it.'

'It's not too bad, really. It's some Italian friends of Stephen's that we met in Rome, something to do with Alfa Romeos, but classy, you know – they had to be asked, Stephen said, but he's gone and got himself tied up in Paris while they're here – and I thought that as you speak Italian better than me, and as we need another girl . . . what do you think?'

'When's it for?'

'The eighteenth.'

'And what for?'

'Oh, just for drinks, I offered dinner but thank God they've got to go to the theatre. Could you make it?'

'It's a very odd request,' I said.

'Yes. I suppose it is. I just didn't want to deal with them, and then . . . '

Her voice trailed away. I was so convinced of ulterior motives that I didn't press the point – especially as she appeared to have conceded it – so I simply agreed to go.

'Oh *thank* you,' she said, 'You are a love . . . Has Francis come home yet?'

'Of course he hasn't. He's not coming till next summer.'

'Lordy Lordy, poor old you. Shall I invite some nice men round for you?'

'What do you think you are, a bawd or a hostess?'

'What an extraordinary remark. If Mama does ring you, you will stand up for me, won't you?'

'I'll do my best. Loulou, why do you think God made people like Daphne? Was it really so that I can be what I am? It hardly seems fair, to say the least.'

'The question's pointless,' she said, lightly. 'London wouldn't be London if it weren't for the provinces. Oxford wouldn't have been Ox if it hadn't been for Redbrick. School wouldn't have been school if it hadn't been for secondary moderns. What can you do about it, except make sure that you come out on top every time?'

'You're right, of course.'

'Of course I am. Truly, Sarah, the Daphnes of this world aren't worth a moment's worry. By worrying about them you get like them and that makes two disasters instead of one. Just sit down and thank God you're you.'

'Oh, I do.'

'Does she still talk about men as boy-friends?'

'I'm afraid so.'

'Oh,' she said, dismissive, 'it isn't even amusing. Ignore it. Give me the flesh eaters, let them all eat each other up, if they can catch each other, and let the others go on chewing the cud . . . I must go, Sarah, see you next week. Cheerio.'

'Cheerio.'

She rang off. I had an extraordinary conviction that my emancipation from her was drawing near: I felt that shortly it would all be over, that I would no longer feel strange and angry at the sound of her voice, or plain and dull in her presence. It was nearly over. This sudden tightness and closeness was the beginning of the end. I felt nearer to understanding her than I had ever been: even her meaningless marriage threatened to float within my vision. I sat down again and looked at the photo of her and John and thought about all that Wilfred had hinted, and I put my money on Louise. She would win. What, I didn't know. But she would win.

I went back to Daphne. I had asked flippantly enough about God's purpose in creating such incomplete creatures, and her answer had been unexpectedly near the bone. I do feel perpetually the double-edged guilt and glory of having so much, so much abundance: at school they tried to argue it out of me by the 'Greater gifts – greater duties to society' line, and I had swallowed it, at least as far as the intellect went – but what on earth was one to do about all this lovely body that one was obliged to walk around with? Skin and limbs and muscle, all glowing and hot with life and energy and hope? Some people haven't got flesh like that, demanding flesh: Daphne is slack and dull, muscles in her legs instead of in her belly, no curves, no shine, no shape, and one can't shut one's eyes and pretend it isn't so, or that, being so, it doesn't matter. It does matter. And yet there is no moral in it. I don't deserve to be as I am: she doesn't deserve to be as she is. And there isn't any way that one can get rid of the guilt of having a nice body by saying that one can serve society with it, because that would end up with oneself as what? There simply doesn't seem to be any moral place for flesh. I didn't worry about all this when Francis was there. Flesh is a straight gift, I concluded: those who have got it had better make the most of this world, because they evidently were created for it and not for the next. I sat there a moment longer, then stood up and looked at myself in the mirror. Myself stared back at myself, caught in a paroxysm of vanity. I hugged my own body in my own arms. My own flesh. Indisputable. Mine.

At lunch-time on the day I went to drinks with Louise I had a very strange experience. It so happened that it was another very cold day, and I put my black stockings on, which I very rarely do as I resent having 'Beatnik' and other insults shouted at me in the street. I got to work without mishap, but in the lunch-hour I went into the nearest W. H. Smith's to buy a packet of envelopes. I was just looking at the paperbacks when a small child aged about three started to stare at me. Her mother tried to distract her, but after a bit the child got loose and wandered over to me, still staring at me entranced. Then – and this is the odd bit – she reached out her little hands and started to pat my legs, and to feel up inside my skirt, along my thighs. I can feel it now, those tiny warm hands on my legs, and the mother in horror saying, 'Pat, come here, Pat.' The child was dragged away, and I smiled, all forgiveness and politeness as ever. I suppose she was puzzled because my legs were black and the rest of me white. I cannot say how strange and primitive those hands felt. My legs seemed to stir to life under them: they began to heave out of their usual careful torpor and to burn under me with an awful warning. Perhaps one perpetually expects larger hands to reach under one's skirt. It was simply the smallness of those that disturbed me.

At Louise's I drank gin and tonic and talked a little bad Italian and soaked myself in the air of worldly well-being that emanated from that flat. Unobtrusive warmth, a choice of drinks, well-deployed lights, cigarettes in all the cigarette-boxes, books on all the bookshelves, and choice duck-egg blue towels on the towel-rails in the bathroom. This really feels like life, I said to myself. It was a pity the people were dull, but then one can't have everything. Anyway, they very shortly left, and left Louise and me confronting each other among the ashtrays. We were talking fairly easily, having been broken in by the presence of others, about films and people and Oxford. She was wearing a lilac-coloured silky jersey. After an idle hour or so, in which we played Frank Sinatra and drank another drink – odd how the very thought of such idle boredom can later cause such pangs of nostalgia and desire – we decided to go and look for something to eat. The kitchen was indeed impressive, as Wilfred had told me at the party – it wasn't in any way modern or streamlined, but very oldy-worldly, with pestles and mortars and jars of herbs and copper pans. It gave the impression of French country cooking. I was pleasantly surprised when Louise opened a cupboard and displayed such normal fare as tins of sardines and beans and ravioli. However, Louise said she felt like cooking, so we had spaghetti: I stood aghast as she tipped wine and garlic recklessly into the sauce, and splashed tomato puree on to her smart shirt affair. Life must be totally different if one doesn't have to think about cleaner's bills. And grocer's bills.

'The funny thing is,' she said, 'that I really love cooking. I'm just greedy, I suppose, but I really love it. The smells and the mixtures. But I won't do it, you know, because it's beneath my dignity. So I have to let Françoise do it most of the time.'

'That's ridiculous. I hate it, and I have to. Let's swap.'

'Why don't you eat out?'

'I don't like eating out alone.'

'Why not?'

'People stare.'

'You little timid. Why don't you just let them?'

'I don't like being stared at. I would like to be ignored.'

'*I* don't mind being stared at.'

'I know. That's because you're always bloody sure of the reason why.'

'Well, what's wrong with that?'

She started to strain the spaghetti through an enormous sieve. I always have to use a small red plastic colander, and everything eels into the sink as often as not. We sat down to eat at the kitchen table, which was covered with a choice orange tablecloth.

'It doesn't go with your blouse,' I said.

'Oh for Christ's sake,' she said furiously. 'You can't have everything matching all the time.'

The spaghetti was most delicious, and when we had finished it we went back into the sitting-room and played Frank Sinatra again. I was struck as we sat there by the charming convention of the scene – sisters idling away an odd evening in happy companionship. It was like something out of *Middlemarch* or even Jane Austen. I was just flicking through the pages of *Harper's* (which was concealed, along with all other papers, in a drawer in a strange off-white cabinet) when she suddenly switched off the gramophone and said, 'Come on, Sarah, let's go out.'

'All right,' I said. 'Where?'

'Let's go and meet John after the theatre.' She looked at her watch. 'He's off in about half an hour. If we get a taxi we'll catch him before he leaves.'

I covered my astonishment and said, 'Won't he mind if I'm there?'

'Why should he mind? Of course he won't. Come on, I can't spend a whole evening in.'

She went and put on her coat, and then said, 'I'd better just make sure I catch him,' and started to make a 'phone call. When she got through she said, 'Hello, is that Bert? . . . This is Mrs Halifax. I wonder if you'd be an angel and tell Mr Connell not to leave unless I'm there . . . yes, I'm coming in to meet him . . . Thank you so much . . . No, that's lovely. So long as you don't let him go.'

I assumed it was the stage door-keeper. There was something naïve in the pleasure which she obviously took in his being called Bert.

'I didn't want to go all the way there and then miss him,' she said to me as she put the receiver down.

We went down the stairs and into the street: it was bitterly cold and I turned my coat collar up round my ears. We had to walk to the main road to pick up a taxi. Louise was remotely exhilarated, as though she were setting out on an adventure. I wondered, as I watched her sideways standing on the street corner waving at the taxi-man with her inimitable, ostentatious grace, whether perhaps she weren't really in love with this man. I had swallowed without a gulp the fact that she didn't, couldn't love Stephen, and the next stage should clearly have been my acceptance of her love for John. But the idea of it didn't convince me. It didn't seem the right explanation. This dim exaltation, this curious breathless-ness, came from some other source. And I seemed nearer to it, as we sat there side by side and watched the big white houses, and then the porticoes of Harrods and all those smart little boutiques off Knightsbridge. Prompted by this sense of impending clarity, I said, 'When you pass clothes in shop windows, could you literally buy everything you see?'

'Everything I want, you mean?'

'Of course.'

'Good Lord no! I mean, there are limits . . . model dresses, and so forth, you know. But most things, I suppose . . .'

'It must be very odd,' I said, trying to prod her into telling me what it really felt like.

'I suppose it is odd, compared with the old days,' she said. 'But it has a curious effect on one, you know . . . I used to like everything I saw, just about, because I couldn't have it . . . and now I scarcely like anything that I see in the shops. They all look sort of imitation . . . you know what I mean. I only want the things I can't have, model dresses and coats and things . . . and one can't really have those. Or not *all* those. And so it goes on. If one had unlimited money, one would find that there simply wasn't a designer good enough in the world. There isn't any top. One thinks there's a top, but there isn't.'

'Doesn't one ever have enough?'

'Never.'

'You can't beat the material world by excess?'

'Ah well,' she said. 'That's an idea, isn't it. I can't say it isn't an idea.'

She paused, smiling at her own reflection in the taxi mirror, as we approached Grosvenor Square. 'Whatever happens,' she went on, 'you can't buy the past. You can't buy an ancestry and a history. You have your own past, and the free will to deal with it, and that's all. It can't be bought with money.' She paused. 'In fact,' she said, irrelevantly, 'Stephen doesn't like some of the clothes I buy. He can't stand this lilac effect. He was furious when my going-away clothes were lilac. Just right for Birmingham, he said, the old snob. So I wear it when he's away. He says it makes me look like a deb. He prefers the classic mode.'

'Why doesn't he like debs?'

'Oh, they're too easy to make fun of – you must have noticed, in his books – no, he doesn't like any social manifestation. He only likes the timeless in his own life.'

'Doesn't he . . . ' I stuck, looking for the right inoffensive word.

'Doesn't he what?'

'Oh, nothing.'

The taxi had reached the streets behind Charing Cross Road, where John's present theatre was. It was very glittering and Christmassy. Louise asked him to drive round to the stage door, and when we got out I didn't offer to pay. There didn't seem to be any point. We had obviously got there before the curtain, as there was no crowd of disgorged spectators thronging the pavement. We went in through the stage door, and Bert, sitting behind a sort of hatch, said, 'Good evening, Mrs H.' It seemed very familiar.

'Evening, Bert,' she said. 'It's very cold out.'

'It's cold enough in,' he said.

'I see we've beaten him to it.'

'Oh yes. He won't be off for another four minutes. It's running a bit late tonight.'

'Good house?'

'Not bad for a Tuesday.'

'Have you had another win yet?'

'No such luck.'

'Bert won seven and sixpence or something stupid on the pools last week,' she said, turning to me. 'Everyone else had filled it in right too.'

'What a shame,' I murmured, dutifully.

'This is my sister, Miss Bennett,' said Louise, and the

man stood up affably and we shook hands. It was all too matey for words, and had a real charm, I am loath to admit. Stage door worlds aren't exactly familiar to me, and I am always rather reluctantly touched by the sentimentality and goodwill and cheek-kissing that goes on. Louise seemed to have taken it in her stride all right. Perhaps the theatrical element in her nature had gravitated naturally to its own level. She certainly would be more at home amongst actresses than amongst female novelists and poets.

After looking at the notice-boards she said, 'Come on, let's go up and give him a surprise.' Again I said that perhaps he wouldn't like my being there, but she brushed this aside as peremptorily as before, and started off up the stairs. They were cold and shabby and bleak, and we seemed to go up for ever.

'I thought he was a star,' I said, crossly. 'Surely they've got a dressing-room further down than this?'

'It's an old theatre,' she said, 'and Hesther's in the one on the floor below.'

When we got there, it said John Connell, Dressing Room 2, on a typewritten slip in the door. Louise pushed it open and a warm fleshy odour of greasepaint and clothes and whisky and sweat met us. It was a small room, but big enough for a *chaise longue* along one wall, which Louise promptly sat on, and lit herself a cigarette. There was a pile of letters at one end of the thing, and she picked them up and started to go through them, just as if I hadn't been there. I sat down on the chair in front of the mirror, and looked at myself, my cheeks and nose inelegantly pink with cold. I dabbed at them with some powder, but to little effect. Then I studied the telegrams and notes stuck all round the mirror. They said things like 'Darling John, all the best for a fabulous success' or 'Darling John, it's going to be a Wow'. There were, as well as the telegrams, a lot of cards portraying bunches of flowers, little ducks, or jokey pictures. There was almost something retarded about the whole thing, to my ignorant eyes. Under the mirror was a litter of Kleenex, cotton wool, powder, sticks of Leichner, and dirty glasses. Also a bottle of whisky, a pretentious-looking book called *Morality and the Middle Classes*, and a lot of old Biros. It was very messy and very human. Quite different from Stephen's meaningless Greek womb. I began to see why Louise fled there so often for refuge. Whatever it lacked, it had life in excess, dirty, exaggerated life. I could hear the play coming over that loudspeaker arrangement: John was blustering on about something or other while Hesther Innes wept or sniffled in the background. It was obviously very near the curtain; indeed, as I listened, John delivered a dying fall, there was a long pause, and muffled clapping broke out. Even before it faded away we heard the noise of feet rushing up the stone stairs, and John broke violently in. He wasn't expecting to see us there, and he stopped on the threshold, panting and dishevelled: but he wasn't an actor for nothing.

'Darling, darling,' he said, and opened his arms to Louise. She got up from the *chaise longue* and walked into them, and they embraced rather lengthily, kissing each other on the lips I noticed. 'Darling, what a marvellous surprise,' he said, as he let her go. 'What are you doing here? And what have you brought Sarah for?' He kissed me too, less effusively, on the cheek.

'I don't know the answer myself,' I said, as it seemed to be me that he was asking. I felt *de trop* in any case, and would willingly have disappeared, if I could have thought of an excuse for doing so. Unfortunately Louise knew I had nothing else to do: I had told her so before the project of theatre visiting had been raised.

'We just came along,' said Louise. 'We were having supper and then we got bored so we just came along. You're pleased to see us, aren't you?'

'Of course, of course. Sit down, I'll be changed in a moment.'

We sat. He really did look pleased to see us – or at least to see Louise. He was obviously excited by her presence: he kept whistling to himself as he washed his hands and started to rub the greasepaint off his face. Their eyes met from time to time in the mirror. I watched him too: in that small space I couldn't pretend to watch anything else. He ripped off his shirt – a white one, but now streaked with brown round the neck and sleeves – and stood there in a string vest as he dabbed at his eyes with cotton wool. His shoulders were huge and covered in black hair. Then he went over to the wash-basin and ran the cold tap: he put his face under it and came up wet and spluttering. Everything he did seemed to make a noise: all his actions were larger and more physical than other men's. I wondered if that was because he was an actor, or whether he was an actor because of that. When he dried himself on a towel, one got the impression that he had just been for a long swim. When he ripped off his trousers I did try to look the other way, but as he seemed quite happy to wander round in his underpants my delicacy seemed out of place, if not positively tactless. He got dressed in his own clothes, which weren't indeed very different from the things he had worn on the stage – the play was about a docker, and John now studiously dressed himself in a check flannel shirt, threadbare round the collar, a pair of dirty jeans, and one of those dark blue dustmen's jackets with leather patches on the shoulders. When he had finished he did look very striking: not quite a docker but far too hefty for a motor-cycling youth. While changing he scarcely said a word: he simply grunted from time to time as he did up a button or reached down to put on his socks. When he was dressed he went over to Louise and stroked her hair and said, 'Well, where shall we go for the evening?'

'You must want something to eat,' she said.

'Oh, I can do without.'

'But we would come with you.'

'Will you? All right then, let's go. After you.'

We filed out again, but on the way down John suddenly said, 'Just a moment, let's go and look at Hesther's baby.'

'Hesther's *what*?' said Louise, as we paused outside Dressing Room 1.

'Hesther's baby. She brought it with her.' He knocked on the door, and the girl inside shouted, 'Come in.' We went in and there was the girl who played opposite John, sitting in a dressing-gown and smoking. She was terribly pretty in a sad, shadowy way, the kind of girl I would have loved to be. She looked a little like a very feminine Simone. John introduced me, and Louise kissed her: 'We've come to look at the baby,' said John.

'Have you really? There he is, in his basket. The girl couldn't get back from her day off today so I brought him with me. Isn't he an angel?'

The baby was lying in a blue basket with pink palm trees on. He was lying on his side, asleep, with his little hands clenched by his mouth. His eyelashes lay on his cheek, enormously long. We were all silent and we could hear him breathing, very lightly and quickly.

'God, he's adorable,' said Louise.

'Has he been asleep all evening?' I asked.

'The whole evening,' she said. 'He went to sleep after I fed him at six, then he slept all the way here in the taxi, and he'll probably sleep all the way back. They're amazing.'

'How old is he?' I asked, entranced.

'Four months.'

'He's so beautiful,' I said.

'He is, isn't he?' she said. I liked her a lot.

When we went out, I said to John, 'What a nice person she is.'

'Isn't she a sweetie?' he said, which wasn't quite what I meant.

'Do they let you just bring a baby to the theatre like that?'

'Why not?'

'It seems so odd – I mean, it seems so easy that there must be some reason against it . . . '

'Oh, there always seem to be babies about in the theatre. I took one on once. It belonged to the wife of one of the extras in *Henry IV* at Oxford, when I was being part of a crowd too, and I took it on.'

'Did it cry?'

'No. It liked it. It smiled at me.' I found myself almost liking John, so touched had I been by his taking us to show the baby and his appreciation of it. I shall never forget the way it lay there with its tiny curled fingers and its skin transparently blossoming, a little pool of absolute stillness and silence in all the dirt and bustle. She remains my image of motherhood, Hesther Innes, with her little baby, sitting in her dressing-gown with a cigarette waiting for the bath. Whenever I think how utterly awful it must be to have a baby I think of her. And yet, someone recently told me, when she found that that baby was on the way she tried to gas herself, and was only saved because her husband got home from work several hours earlier than she expected him. She was afraid that the baby would ruin her career. But the baby won, it existed, and when I think of mothers and babies I nevertheless think of her.

When we got outside, after bidding Bert goodnight, it was colder than ever. John put his arm round Louise, and I remembered how warm and comforting it was when Francis used to put his arm round me on a cold night. I felt acutely lonely: everyone had lovers and babies and husbands but me. But the loneliness didn't make me feel miserable: I almost enjoyed it, as the dreary edge was taken off the sensation by the darkness and glamour of the night, and the strangeness of being with my sister and her man. Nothing so strange is ever really unbearable.

We were walking towards Covent Garden, through those old streets that feel like the most ancient part of London. A lot of the West End is just like any other large city, but more ugly: but the courts and inns and markets have a history and a flavour of their own. Walking along a road like Long Acre, I can imagine Dr Johnson up at night with nowhere to sleep, or drinking with Beauclerk, or visiting actresses or Garrick in the Green Room after the show. I can picture centuries of people coming out of Drury Lane with their husbands and lovers, to talk about the play and to go thankfully, idly, for a drink. Theatrical life has such continuity, as does the life of selling vegetables, because, despite cinemas and frozen foods, the main product is ephemeral and always in demand. So Covent Garden and Drury Lane go on, next door to each other, and though the details change, the way of life is the same. I realized, as we walked there, that what Louise was doing was a reversal of roles: she was taking the man's part, calling at the theatre instead of being called for. She was in the tradition, but she had reversed it, instead of opting out completely, as most girls are now obliged to do. I felt a glow of admiration: she was, after all, striking a blow for civilization in her behaviour, not, as it first had seemed, for anarchy. Why that should be admirable I didn't go into, but I was sure it was: it was braver than to abandon the game completely. To force marriage into a mould of one's own, while still preserving the name of marriage – it seemed an enterprise worth consideration. Indeed, there was almost something classic in her position, something more deeply rooted in the shapes of life than the eternal triangle of a woman's magazine. Her position was certainly a lot more classic than mine, and therefore more beautiful and more gracious: mine, I couldn't help feeling, was a truly unprecedented mess, which no girl before this century could ever have landed herself in. No doubt I over-emphasize my isolation, but there can be no doubt that Louise herself realized that she was part of an unbroken line, rather than a freak. And she drew real pleasure from that concept, as she drew pleasure from the idea of Grosvenor Square, and model dresses, and entertaining.

Louise and John were discussing where to eat. John, apparently, had a leaning towards egg and chips, which Louise hadn't.

'The thing is,' Louise was saying, 'that you only like the *idea* of it, and when you get there you always say the food is greasy or the tables are dirty. You might just as well go somewhere clean.'

'Well, where?'

'There must be lots of places.'

'Of course, we're quite near the Waldorf,' he said, mocking.

'What about Rossi's?'

'You are odd, that's just as dirty as all the egg and chip caffs.'

'Yes, but it doesn't look it.'

'That's true.'

'Foreign dirt is all right, somehow.'

'Well, so long as we know where we're going. It's freezing.'

As we quickened our step I found myself wondering what sort of place Rossi's was – I couldn't picture Louise and John going to such an utterly ordinary place as it turned out to be. When we got there, it was nothing but one of those tiny coffee bars with Espresso machines and plants in pots, and a menu with Spaghetti Bolognaise, 3s 6d; Veal Escalope, 5s 6d; Ghoulash, 4s 6d. It was very crowded, but we found an uncomfortable little corner and settled in – the seats were rooted to the ground. As if anyone wanted to steal chairs. The other two seemed to

181

know half the clientèle, who were all obviously actors and hangers-on – I was amazed by the easy familiarity with which everyone treated Louise. She was evidently a well-established fact. The terms of her relationship with John were now completely unambiguous, and I wondered how I could ever have doubted the state of affairs between them. They held hands under the table and kicked each other in the leg from time to time: they made jokes with undertones, and from one or two remarks I gathered that this had been going on for some time. Wilfred had hinted that it started before Louise married, I remembered. They were undoubtedly a very striking couple, and fitted together very well – both tall, and dark and sexy, both strange and affected in their clothes, though choosing different affectations. They looked by Louise's own definition, very predatory. For some reason they seemed to enjoy my company, and I guessed, from watching them, that they needed an audience to build up the striking, wicked image of themselves. In fact, I was playing at being a herbivore for a while, and gazing with admiration into the dangerous caves of the fiercer breed. I didn't mind. It soothed my conscience. Perhaps I am a herbivore at heart, and only predatory by conviction.

In fact, I was so content to sit quiet and play at being an impressionable chaperone that I was taken aback when Louise and John actually started to talk about me and to ask me questions. They asked me about my job, and I felt mildly flattered, and replied as though to a kind aunt who had taken me out to tea and asked me obligatory, con-versational things about school and lessons.

'But do you find it satisfying?' asked John. 'Really satisfying?'

'Of course I don't,' I said, deciding to abandon the 'It's-very-interesting' line I had hitherto pursued. 'Of course it's not satisfying. It's so pointless that I can't even think what I do do all day. It's one of those time-fillers. It bears about the same relation to anything I want to do as painting backcloths must bear to painting canvases – '

'Then why the hell don't you get out of it?'

'And into what? Suggest something else. And I will. Suggest me something nearer my heart's desire that will also pay the rent and I'll be off tomorrow.'

'I never understood,' said Louise, vaguely, 'why you didn't stay on at Oxford.'

'Doing what?'

'Oh, research and so forth . . . '

'Did you ever take a look at all the people who *did* stay on and do research and so forth? Because they're my reason. I like the place and I like the work but I don't like the people. I wouldn't like to be one of those. It's the same with teaching.'

'There must be something you want to do.'

'Why?'

'Well, there usually is.'

'Oh, there are hundreds of things I want to *do*,' I said, casting my mind over them – things like going to Rome, or seeing Francis and loving him as I used to, and having the right clothes for everything, and writing books – 'but you couldn't call any of them careers. You couldn't earn a penny from any of them.'

'You haven't had time to settle down yet,' said John.

'I never will settle down,' I said. 'There simply isn't a niche for me.'

'What are all your friends doing?' said Louise.

'Oh, don't ask. They're all making as atrocious a mess of it as me. Wandering around America or the Continent wishing they had something better to do, or married and bored, or teaching in secondary moderns – God, you can take the lot for me.'

'I've always rather fancied you as a don,' said Louise.

'I used to fancy myself as one. But I'll tell you what's wrong with that. It's sex. You can't be a sexy don. It's all right for men, being learned and attractive, but for a woman it's a mistake. It detracts from the essential seriousness of the business. It's all very well sitting in a large library and exuding sex and upsetting everyone every time your gown slips off your bare shoulders, but you can't do that for a living. You'd soon find yourself having to play it down instead of up if you wanted to get to the top, and when you've only got one life that seems a pity.'

'I agree,' said John. 'You should try acting. That's what it's about.'

'I would if I could. It must be fun, letting rip in public like that.'

Louise was strangely silent at this point, no doubt thinking back. I wondered if she regretted her own decisions. After a while she said, 'Wilfred Smee said he talked to you at our party.'

'Yes, he did.'

'Do you like Wilfred?'

'Yes, I do. It would be all right being a don if one could be like that. I mean to say, with him the question is altogether different.'

'Don't you think he could be very boring?' said John. 'When he gets older and more out of touch with things?'

'Out of touch with what?'

'Oh, the world . . . '

'The *world*,' I said, scornfully, having had about enough of that concept both from myself and from Louise. 'Oh yes, the world, of course, I forgot about that . . . '

'What he means,' said Louise, 'is interesting people like himself. He wonders what poor old Wilfred will be like when he's cut off from that great representative of the inner ring, John What's-His-Name.'

'I've always thought,' I said, 'that very few people grow old as admirably as academics. At least books never let them down.'

'Tell me,' said John, 'what would you really like to achieve most in your life?'

'I'll tell you,' I said. 'Beyond anything I'd like to write a funny book. I'd like to write a book like Kingsley Amis, I'd like to write a book like *Lucky Jim*. I'd give the world to be able to write a book like that.'

'Do you really mean it?'

'Of course I mean it.'

He laughed. 'God,' he said, 'you really are a little egg-head, aren't you. You really are.'

'Well, I don't like the word you choose,' I said, 'but as to the idea, I must admit that however hard I run away from it, you're probably absolutely right. But if you think that that implies that my right place is sitting in some library, you couldn't be more wrong . . . ' And even as I spoke a great wave of nostalgia came over me, nostalgia for days at a library desk with a pile of books and an essay subject and a week to find the answer, and the prospect of someone to tell me I was right or wrong, and the thought of exams to pass and knowledge to discover, which now seemed not to exist, or not in any discoverable form. Oh hell, I said to myself, and shut my mind on the idea. Only a real idiot would use the thought of a library as an image of the womb.

They talked about Wilfred a bit, and I tried hard to work out what that strange trio all thought of each other, but after a while I noticed that both John and Louise were getting unnervingly amorous. I was relieved when they said, 'Come on, let's go,' and jumped up willingly. But they weren't going to let me off so easily: they insisted that I walked down to the Strand with them and accepted a lift home in their taxi.

'It's miles out of your way,' I said, 'absolutely miles, it'll cost you a fortune to take me back first.'

'As a matter of fact,' said John, 'I live on the way there, you can drop me off if that would satisfy your conscience.'

'Don't be silly,' said Louise to John.

'I'm not being,' he said. 'I simply don't believe you. He's sure to have changed his mind and then we would be in a mess.'

'I promise you,' said Louise.

For reply, he kissed her, right there in the street.

'For God's sake,' I said, 'do you mind waiting till you've delivered me on my doorstep?'

'All right,' said Louise. She was laughing to herself, and skipping on the pavement, avoiding the cracks. I envied her bitterly at that moment. It seemed that she had everything and love as well. Everything shall be added unto you, as Jesus Christ once said. Seek ye first the kingdom of this world and everything shall be added unto you. What a bribe. And I said to myself, Louise always wins. Whatever she does, she wins. And I lose. I've too much wit and too little beauty, so I lose.

When we reached the Strand we picked up a taxi, and once we were in it out of the cold Louise threaded her arms round John's waist under his dustman's jacket and started saying silly things like 'Keep me warm, little bear, keep me warm.' They couldn't think of anything but the night ahead in Stephen's empty flat, and they were taking me home to tease themselves, to push away the hour of arrival. I'd never seen Louise childish before, and it reminded me of how childish Francis and I always were at our most happy moments: I think the most enchanting thing he ever said to me was that my nipples were like jelly-babies. Nobody else could ever have said as beautiful and stupid a thing as that. I began to feel all strung up with loneliness as I watched them billing and cooing, so to speak. I, of course was sitting on one of the foldable seats so that they could recline on the back seat together. I can't tell you how I longed to be lying on that back seat with somebody. With almost anybody. By the time we rolled up at my front door, I was, to be crude for a welcome change, twitching. I got out, and they said good night, their mutual satisfaction overflowing into benevolence, and I thought how easy it is to be kind when everything is going right and one isn't dying of many varieties of frustration. The thought of my empty bed appalled me. I waved good-bye to them, and unlocked the front door, and thought how sad it was that I had only found it amusing to be a bachelor girl for a week at the most. I hadn't much independence, I thought. And those stupid home truths about a woman being nothing without a man kept running through my head as I groped my way up the unlit stairs.

I tried to be as quiet as possible in order not to wake Gill, as I didn't want to talk to her, but I needn't have worried. On the kitchen table there was a letter from her, underneath the dripping bowl. It said:

Dear Sarah,

I seem to have thrown the sponge in at last. I'm going home for a while. I didn't feel too well this morning, so I rang them up and they asked me to go home. Perhaps I'll get over everything quicker if I go home. I know I've been pretty impossible recently, but things have been a strain. I hope it won't cause a rift. I've left the week's rent in the jar on the mantelpiece – I hope you'll find someone else to share with. I am sorry about everything. If Tony calls, tell him where I am.

Yours, Gill

As I put the letter down I felt as if I could burst into tears. It was so sad, that a girl like Gill should be beaten simply because she had taken a gamble on love. Because that did seem to be the reason. She had jumped in with her eyes shut, and she had got nowhere. I began to wonder if I myself would ever dare to get married. There were so many dangers. Not that Francis would ever do what Tony had done, or ever be what Stephen was, but then who did that leave me as my model? My parents? Cosy

Michael and Stephanie? Oh, I didn't want it, any of it. I felt frightened and ill. Frightened, ill, and yet desirous. I wondered if Gill and Tony would have been all right if they had had as much money as Louise and Stephen. Then none of the squalor, put-the-kettle-on problem would ever have arisen. But other things would. Other things would. I was in despair, and lonely too. Perhaps the only way to do it was to marry and then to have affairs. Like Louise, my sister. But I didn't want to, I didn't want to do that, I wanted to be a one-man girl, and faithful. It was impossible.

I didn't burst into tears: I started to wander around restlessly, feeling the objects in the room, looking at myself in the mirror, eating a lump of cheese. I felt that I must do something, talk to someone. Some man. I tried to think of somebody, and in the end I remembered Jackie Almond. I knew I had his telephone number, and I found it in my address book. I rang him up, without stopping to think how late it was: he was in, and I asked him to come round. He didn't seem surprised at my request: he simply said he would come. I suppose that from his one encounter with me he must have formed an impression of me which would make such eccentric behaviour far more in character than it actually was. I daresay he was the sort of person that sad, high-powered chance acquaintances were always ringing up in the middle of the night for help and comfort. Anyway, in half an hour he came. We settled down on the hearthrug, holding hands and drinking Maxwell House: I don't know in what direction we were heading, because just as I was settling down into a warm, companionable and harmless embrace the 'phone rang.

'Damn, damn, damn,' I said. 'Who the hell can that be at this time of night?'

'Don't answer it,' he said. This I took to be an indication of affection, so I didn't answer it. But it went on and on ringing, until on the twenty-sixth ring I felt I had to reply. I thought it might be an accident.

I lifted up the receiver and said my number crossly.

'Sarah, is that you?' It was Louise.

'Louise,' I said, furiously, and speaking straight to her for the first time in my life. 'Louise, what in God's name do you mean by ringing people up at this unspeakable hour of night. I've never heard of anything so absurd.'

'Look, Sarah, I'm terribly sorry to have woken you,' she said, agitated, on the other end of the line. 'I couldn't think what to do. The most awful unspeakable thing has happened. It's too incredible for words, I simply can't believe it . . . ' She sounded tremulous, and her voice faded away.

'You mean you're going to have a baby?' I said, snappily, as this was the sort of event that usually calls forth such incredulous clamour. And it was time in the story for that to happen to someone, at least in such a female love-love-love story as this.

'Oh no,' she said, brightly catching my tone of voice – she's not slow, my sister – 'nothing as corny as that, but just as stupid. You know I went back to the flat with John – well, we were just sitting in the bath together when in walks Stephen. Can you imagine? I sort of knew he would, somehow. It was too awful for words.'

I wanted badly to laugh, but I knew it would be tactless. I could see how utterly awful it would be – exposure is bad enough under any circumstances, but when accompanied by an atmosphere of wet sponges and toothbrushes it must be really humiliating. There is after all something classic about a bed, something dignified and timeless. But a bath . . .

'What on earth did he say?' I said.

'Oh God, it was ghastly . . . he went absolutely ill with rage, I've never seen anything like it, none of that turn the other cheek lark he's been so keen on all his life. I thought they were going to hit each other, but then with all that nakedness . . . anyway John walked out and left me to it, and I got dry and put my dressing-gown on and then Stephen came back and he gave me such a thing – he's mad, Sarah, I'm telling you, he's really mad. And then he locked me out of the house.'

'How long ago was all this?'

'About ten minutes.'

'Where are you then?'

'I'm in the 'phone box on the corner. I borrowed four-pence from the taxi-man to see if you were in . . . can I come round, Sarah, please?'

'Oh God,' I said. 'You couldn't have picked a worse night. Can't you go to someone else?'

'I couldn't tell anyone else, I really couldn't . . . '

'Oh come off it, Louise, we're not exactly intimate friends, are we?'

'You're my sister,' she said, bleakly.

'Oh for Christ's sake. Why don't you ring up John? You can't come here.'

'I couldn't ring him. I couldn't.'

'Why on earth not?'

'Isn't it obvious?'

'Not particularly.'

'Well, if you must know, I tried to ring him just a minute ago, but either he isn't in or he didn't answer. Please let me come, Sarah, I'm catching my death of cold. I'll love you for ever more if you'll let me come.'

'It's cold here too,' I said.

'Yes, but you're not standing in your dressing-gown,' she said.

'True,' I admitted. Then what she had said registered and I said, 'Why, are you?'

'That's right. I've got nothing on except my dressing-gown. And I haven't got a penny – I'll have to borrow the taxi money from you when I arrive, if the taxi-man hasn't raped me on the way.'

'I said you couldn't come,' I said. I enjoyed, in a simple way, the feeling of power.

'You've got to let me come,' said Louise. 'There's no one else I dare ask.'

'Go back and ask Stephen. I'm sure he'd let you in.'

'I'm never going near that man again,' she said, classically. 'He gives me the creeps. I can't stand the sight of him. I'll never touch another penny of his money. I'll never speak to him again. I hate him, I hate him, I hate him.'

'Oh, OK,' I said, as thoughts of the police and Louise in her dressing-gown all over the *Daily Express* began to flit through my mind. 'Oh, OK, I suppose you can come, as long as you realize that you won't be very welcome. That I'm doing you a favour. How long will you be?'

'Just as long as the taxi takes. Bless you, Sal. Will you come down with the taxi money if I ring the bell when I get there?'

'You really are the bloody limit. All right.'

'I know I am. I'll be seeing you.'

I rang off. I was annoyed; curious, admittedly, but annoyed. I was annoyed on account of Jackie, who was part of my life: I was furious with her for her assumption that she could just come round and impose her life on me whenever she wanted. And the truth was that up till then she always had been able to: she had been expert at using me and impressing me without my noticing it. And this time I had noticed: I noticed and I genuinely, truly resisted. As I went and sat down by Jackie something very very old snapped in me. It snapped as though it had been a piece of old and rotten string, long useless, long without any power to tie, and yet still wrapped round and confining an ancient parcel of fears and prejudices. It snapped, and the parcel spilled apart all over the floor.

'Who on earth was that?' said Jackie.

'That was my sister Louise,' I said. 'She's coming round here in her dressing-gown as her husband has thrown her out on the streets.'

'I told you not to answer the phone.'

'Yes, I know. I'm sorry.'

'I don't suppose it matters very much. I'd better go.'

'I don't want you to go.'

'I don't want to go either.'

'But you'd better.'

'Yes.'

'It isn't that you are less important than my sister. In fact, you're being here now has made all the difference to everything. Your being here when she rang, I mean.'

'Thank you.'

'I mean it, Jackie. The end of something is at hand.'

'You're a little obscure.'

'I can't explain it. But the fact that I would rather sit here with you than let her come here means a lot.'

'But you let her come just the same.'

'I didn't want to.'

'Then why did you?'

'Because she – because blood is thicker than water, I suppose.'

'I too have blood in my veins.'

'I know. That is the principle I have always worked on. That everyone has blood in their veins. Everyone except Louise, that is. But now I begin to realize that she has too. And the point is that although I let her come I didn't want her to come.'

'I take your point,' he said.

And then he got up and put on his coat. I didn't feel bad about having let him come, so magnificently sure of myself did I feel. Of myself *versus* Louise. And I didn't feel bad about letting him go. All I hoped was that he realized how important it was that he had been there. I think he did.

We said good-bye and made another rendezvous, an outdoor one this time. Then we kissed and he went and I began to wait for Louise.

When the doorbell went I picked up my purse with the taxi money and went downstairs. There was my amazing sister, standing on the doorstep in a short grey dressing-gown, looking not nearly as disastrous as I had expected, because her dressing-gown resembled a sort of maternity coat rather than a piece of sprigged Victoriana. I gave her the money for her fare, which she gave to the taxi-man, who made some joke at which she vaguely laughed. He drove off, waving and shouting, 'Don't catch a chill,' and Louise came in shivering and clutching her dressing-gown frantically around her. Her legs looked white and naked underneath: usually she wears dark stockings. 'What story did you tell him?' I asked, as I followed her up the stairs. 'Oh, I told him most of the truth,' she said, over her shoulder. 'He liked it, he thought it was funny. I suppose you think it's funny. I suppose it is funny.'

'Oh no,' I said, shutting the door after her as we reached the top. 'It isn't funny except for the bit about the bath. That was funny. Here, sit down and get warm. Shall I make you a cup of Maxwell House?'

'Have you any cocoa?'

'We might have.' I went into the kitchen and looked. We hadn't. I put some coffee in a cup instead. My cup and Jackie's were still sitting side by side on the hearth: I wondered if she would notice them, but of course she didn't. It had never crossed her mind that I had any real reason for not wanting her to come. This wasn't sur-prising. I don't think she ever speculated much about my life. Or if she did, I doubt if she guessed right. Just as I so often guessed wrong about her. I had to ask her everything in questions.

She looked quite normal, very pale and un-made up, and one couldn't have told from her appearance that anything was wrong, except for a violent uncontrolled shivering that she indulged in from time to time. Part of it was, I suppose, the cold, but part of it must have been neurotic. She looked oddly as though she were taking part in a college cocoa party, sitting there undressed and drinking a mug of coffee. Now for a tête-à-tête, I said to myself, and I asked her, 'Well, what are you going to do next?'

'I don't know,' she said. 'I don't know where to go.'

'Do you really mean that you're not going back to Stephen?'

'Certainly I mean it. I'm never going near him again. Nor am I ever going home again. I'm truly finished off this time.'

By home she meant our parents' home.

'Well,' I said, 'you must have got plenty of money. You can go where you like.'

I find it hard to believe that anyone who has a lot of money can really be in a fix, though I am obviously wrong. 'Why,' I said, 'you could go abroad tomorrow, you could go anywhere you wanted. I quite envy you,' I said, trying to cheer her up.

'Do you realize that every penny I have belongs to that man?'

'To Stephen?'

'Yes. To Stephen.'

'What's the matter with Stephen? Why have you gone off him so suddenly?'

'Oh, for God's sake, I was never on him. You can't pretend you like him either so don't bother trying. Nobody likes him.'

'Well, well, well. Then what did you marry him for?' I asked, thinking with delight that at very long last we had got down to brass tacks, and congratulating myself on asking the question I had been itching to ask for months.

'Oh Lordy,' said Louise, 'you must be the only person in the world who doesn't know the answer to that question. I married him for his money, of course.'

'Did you really?' I was full of shock and admiration.

'Of course I did. What other attraction do you think he could have for anyone?'

'But Loulou, what a terribly wicked thing to do.'

'Is it really wicked? I suppose it is. It's beginning to me to seem rather the normal thing to do. Though I must say I surprised myself, once, long ago, when I first made my mind up. Yes, I really took myself by surprise. But that was so long ago.'

'Good Lord,' I said, 'how ignorant I must be. I think you're the only person I know who married for money. I know they're always doing it in books but I thought it was just a novelist's convention. Do you think all those other things like wicked stepmothers are true too? All the fairy-story things?'

'I think it's more than likely,' said Louise, having another energetic shiver.

'Have a blanket,' I said.

'No thank you. I'm not cold.'

'Do go on then, this is fascinating, tell me when you decided to take this awful step. When did you decide to marry him? Did he keep asking you?'

'He asked me every day. I don't know when I decided. I think it was somewhere round about the time when I came to see you in Oxford last term. Do you remember when John and Stephen and I came? It was something about the way Stephen kept paying all the bills. Perhaps you didn't notice. Wherever I go with Stephen, there are always a thousand bills, and he pays for everything, and I know it doesn't matter. With John it sometimes mattered, but with Stephen it never did. It was like suddenly realizing that the Americans might wipe out Russia, and then one would have no more worries about war. That would be immoral, and tragic, but it would be safe. Have you ever thought that? That they might one night just wipe the whole lot out, and we would live in our lifetimes. And it was the same with money. I suddenly realized that if I married Stephen I need never think about need or want again. About wanting things I couldn't buy.'

'Did you always want so many things you couldn't have?'

'Oh, desperately. Don't you? Partly it's looking the way I do. I must have clothes. I'm only young once, as they say, and I'm already twenty-four, and if I don't have the clothes now I'd feel I wasn't paying a debt to nature. And other things like food and theatres. I felt I must have them.'

'I feel I must have them, but I tell myself I'm wrong for feeling that way. Didn't you feel you were being wicked?'

'Wrong. Wicked. I don't know, I really don't. All those books I used to read, and I could never work out the simplest thing from them, like whether it was better to be a virgin or not. And then I was so serious at heart. I got so sick of people thinking I was serious. Do you think it was so awful a thing to do, Sal?'

'Don't be silly,' I said. 'I think it's rather a thrilling thing to do, to marry for money.'

'You are a baby,' she said, grandly and wanly: I could see that my enthusiasm was having an excellent and tonic effect on her. 'It isn't thrilling at all, it's rather a cynical thing to do.'

'Well, I think it's rather grand to be cynical. Rather classy. I'm far too ignorant to be cynical.'

'If you insist on my choosing a non-grand word for

myself, then I should say that what I did was just plain feeble. I did it because I didn't trust people.'

'Didn't trust who?'

'Men.'

'Oh. I think I trust men as much as I trust women, don't you?'

She laughed, and then sneezed. 'That's not the point,' she said.

'Why did you get married in such a hurry?'

'I felt I had to get it over. And Stephen insisted so.'

'Tell me about Stephen. Why was he so keen on marrying you? What kind of man is he to live with?'

'I couldn't begin to tell you about him. He's too horrid, you wouldn't believe how horrid and awful he is. He's a nut-case, but the most selfish, the most specious, the most mean kind of maniac that was ever let loose . . . I'm not sure that it wasn't quite straightforwardly all that money that helped to ruin him, you ought to hear him talking about our daily, he talks about her as though she weren't human. Nothing but a comic creature that says funny things. I know you and I are pretty hopeless with that kind of person, but with me it's because I'm frightened of them, I'm aware the whole time of how overwhelmingly human they are. She's a spinster, our daily, and she had a budgie that died. Stephen laughed when she went on about it, and said Poor old Miss McGregor, but I wasn't so dead to all human feeling not to realize that to her that bird was like a child. And if that's funny then everything is. Everything.'

'Doesn't he realize about some people not having money?'

'No, not at all. He knows, but he doesn't realize. He's always criticizing the clothes of the people we know – or rather the people I know – it makes me wild. He doesn't think that certain styles and certain colours cost a lot of money. All the brilliant social satire people manage to detect in his books is nothing more nor less than his own bitchy snobbism. He's an articulate snob. He doesn't understand, he sneers.'

'I could have guessed that from his books. They lack compassion.'

'How beautifully, how lit. critically you put it. They do.'

'What on earth did he use to think about my clothes then?'

'He hates the way your shoes are always down-at-heel. But on the whole he thinks you're picturesque.'

I laughed. 'Charming,' I said. 'And where does he get all his taste and money from?'

'That's another thing. He pretends he's making all his money out of his books, but of course he isn't, he couldn't keep himself in socks off them. He lives off his father's tobacco factory or whatever it is. You should hear his double-thinks on lung cancer, they have to be heard to be believed. And he pretends his family are part of the Halifax family, which is just a bloody lie as they have no connexions at all. Not that I would mind about that if it weren't that he didn't. I have to tread so carefully, it's like dealing with a baby. Oh God, he's such a liar.'

'You haven't told me why he married you.'

'I really don't know. I thought he wanted to because he loved me – he used to go on and on about how much he loved me, and how I was the most beautiful woman in the world, which I was only too ready to believe, and how important it was that I should marry him . . . he made me feel it was my duty to marry him, so it wasn't all money and self-interest, a tiny bit of it was a feeling of pity and obligation on my part. But do you know what all that long love-nonsense was? Nothing but a seduction. Would you credit it? Talk about wicked to marry for money, think of the shock when you find somebody has actually set out to seduce you in a totally hypocritical and methodical way, not meaning a word of it but just wanting to get you into bed or in his case to the altar which for him came to the same thing. It's like something out of *Les Liaisons Dangereuses*. And when he gets you there he's more or less incapable, not that that has anything to do with it. Oh God. Oh God. I knew I was breaking some kind of rule of the heart, but I don't think I deserve to end up with a husband that made me feel sick.'

'In what way . . . ?' I began, tentatively, but she stopped me with, 'Don't ask me about that, just don't ask me, that's all. He hurt me, if you want to know. He hurt me.'

I didn't want to know.

'When did you begin to find all this out?' I asked.

'Far later than I should have done. Far too late. When we married I just thought he was a bit odd. I really believed it when he said he loved me. I thought he was a nut, but quite a kind and sad and interesting one. But later . . . Oh, Sarah, I was so bored. So crashingly, terrifyingly bored. You can't imagine anything like it. It wasn't that he suddenly changed, or anything like that, it was just that I saw too much of him and too little of anyone else. It was being abroad that did it, because all the people we ever saw were his friends, or rather his business contacts, and I had to spend hour after hour, meal after meal being civil to people in order to get them to do obscure things for him. I don't think he wanted to come home because he wanted to hang on to me. And he knew that out there in Rome and Paris I couldn't really get away.'

'Couldn't you wander off sometimes?'

'Oh yes. I wasn't a prisoner. And although he's jealous he's not tyrannical. But it was so difficult to meet anyone. All I ever seemed to meet were waiters. I ran across Michael in Paris, and I even envied him.'

'It must be odd, being abroad with a lot of money.'

'It is odd. In some way it kills desire. It pads one from the sharpness of everything.'

'But in Paris you saw John?'

'Yes. John flew over one night after the show, one Saturday night. It was terrible. We wanted to go out together, but I was too worn down by this time to do anything outrageous, so we all three went out to dinner on the Saturday night, very late. We went to a nightclub, which was at least something – you know how Stephen hates drink and places where people drink, unless he's going to get something out of it. But he and John talked the whole time, about contracts and this bloody film, which is a real non-starter, and in the end I said couldn't John and I have a dance together. So we did, and he's so bloody you know what, but for some reason my pride wouldn't let me say what a bad time I was having, and he was furious with me. He always hated the idea of my marrying Stephen.'

'That's not surprising.'

'No, it's not.' She looked amused at the thought: she was still intrigued and faintly impressed by the absurdity of what she had done.

'You know,' she said, 'I've recently begun to think that Stephen's in love with John himself, and won't admit it, or else has admitted it to John and been told what John the darling would immediately tell him. So when he saw that he had a chance of getting me, when I was what John wanted, it must have seemed to him a chance of evening off a lot of old scores, and of getting a sort of vicarious satisfaction at the same time.'

'I used to think Stephen was queer,' I said.

'As well as everything else. I don't know why he's spent so much of his life and time running after girls. I've only found out about all the others quite recently. There was a girl called Sappho that I met at a party. We were very tight, and she told me the whole story, and then she sent me the letters he had written her. And would you credit it, there was a lot of it word for word the same as he wrote to me? Have you ever heard of anything so criminal?'

'Never,' I said. It was appalling to think of her, such a first-hand beauty, being dished out second- and third-hand phrases, even by somebody she didn't love. I tried to imagine what it would have done to my vanity, let alone hers.

'Honestly,' she went on, 'you wouldn't believe what a morass of duplicity that man is. He sins against every kind of human relationship I can think of. You remember how seriously we used to take all these things at Oxford, truth and honesty and being subtle with people and not trampling on feelings? I used to spend days worrying about how to refuse an invitation. And then to meet someone who has all the jargon of it and none of the reality, with no more idea of what it's about than an elephant . . . oh, when I married him I thought we were going to be sophisticated all right, me marrying him for his money, and he unrequitedly but gratefully worshipping me, and me straightforwardly and nobly and honestly admitting that I didn't love him – and I never said I did, never – and me straightforwardly and nobly going off with John, and us all sitting and discussing these things cleverly over large drinks – God, what a fool I was, what fools women are, what fools middle-class girls are to expect other people to respect the same gods as themselves and E. M. Forster . . . anyway, I'm through with it all now, through with all that.'

'Through with all what?' I asked, as I realized that what she was saying was that all these childish idols of truth and honesty were real, and she answered, 'Oh, through with all that money and duplicity.'

'I don't understand why you didn't marry John instead of Stephen. Or didn't he ask you?'

'He did ask me. In a way. He would have married me. He was mad about me.'

'Then why didn't you marry him? He's got plenty of money.'

'He has at the moment, but he spends it like water, and you never can tell with actors. He may be out of work for years.'

'You are a right bitch, aren't you,' I said, admiringly.

'And also I don't really love him very much – oh, love, love, I know one oughtn't to drag it in, but I really don't love John enough to marry him. To put up with all that being married means. And I know that he'd be unfaithful if we did marry and I don't love him little enough to enjoy that, so you see that it wouldn't have worked . . .'

'You mean, in fact, that you love him but you don't trust him,' I said.

She was taken aback. She stopped in her outpouring to consider the proposition.

'I never thought about not trusting him. I think it's unlikely that he loves me more than any of his other women.'

'Why?'

'Why should he?'

'Oh, Louise,' I said, from the depths of my experience. 'That's no way to talk about love.'

And I meant it. I thought of Tony and I said, 'Just because he's got a lot of other women doesn't mean he doesn't love you. Can't you tell? I thought I could, earlier tonight. How did he react when you decided to marry Stephen?'

'He was furious. But I didn't pay it much attention, I didn't see why I should pay him any more respect than he paid me. There's something about his being an actor that prevents me from taking anything he does seriously. Now Stephen, he's quite different, writers have always been known for a sensitive lot . . . '

'It just shows how wrong you can be . . . have you been seeing much of John since you got back from Paris?'

'Nearly every day.'

'But didn't Stephen notice?'

'I don't know what he noticed or didn't notice. He must have realized that it was impracticable to try and keep me away from people here – he was always going out himself, he couldn't very well ask me for my itinerary. And in a way it was his lack of interest that annoyed me. His lack of superficial interest, I mean. I'm sure he was seething away inside, but he never asked me just sort of casually where I had dinner or what film I'd been to see. Even when I quite wanted to talk about it. I suppose he was afraid to broach the subject. Just in case.'

'Did he talk to you?'

'Not much. He had this thing about having to be quiet when he worked – not that he was working at anything, except this film script. He kept ringing up his director in Paris. It gives me quite a kick to think of that 'phone bill. I used to ring people up all over the country, everyone I could think of. When I was alone in the evenings. And people were always ringing him up too, business people and publishers and tobacco factory people about shares. They used to think I was his secretary and give me messages. In the end I had to be quite rude, and say I was his wife and not there to write notes for him. All they ever said was that they didn't know he was married. That did give me a lift, believe me! It made me feel really important.'

'Couldn't you see all this coming?'

'I told you. I thought I'd be free, to have my cake and eat it. To keep love as a sideline. Don't you ever marry for love, Sarah. It does terrible things to people.'

So does the other thing, I thought, but I asked, 'Why? Why do you say that?'

'Do you remember Stella?'

'Stella Conroy?'

'That's right.'

I did remember Stella. She had been the same year as Louise, though at Cambridge, not Oxford: she was as much the Oxford type as Louise wasn't, blonde, soft, very slightly whimsy, a beauty *au naturel*. They had been close friends ever since they had met at interview-time on Bletchley station, smoking their first cigarettes. She had several friends in Oxford and used to come across from time to time: also, she had been to stay with our family more than once. She was the kind of friend who is invaluable with parents: totally reliable as far as charm, deference and cleanliness are concerned. I doubt if anyone who knew her ever disliked her.

'Yes,' I said, 'I remember Stella.'

'You know she married Bill?'

'Bill?'

'The physics man she knew. They got married the year they came down, a week after the end of term or something dotty. And now they've got two babies.'

'How super,' I said, automatically, but Louise cried almost with frenzy, 'No, it isn't, it isn't super at all, it's the worst catastrophe I've ever seen.'

She stopped for a moment, and then she said, more calmly, 'What's happened to me is bliss compared with that. You ought to go and visit them. They live in a slum in Streatham, and Bill lectures at the Polytechnic, and Stella goes mad with that baby – there was only one when I saw them. They didn't mean to have them, either of them, and poor Stella hasn't even the comfort of hating them because she's incapable of hate. She wouldn't know how to hate them.'

'When did you see all this?'

'I went to see them last spring, when she was expecting her second – it was too terrible, the baby was sitting on its pot and screaming, and the loo was littered with wet nappies, and everywhere smelt of babies. There were plastic toys all over the place, and you could hardly get through the front door for the pram, and there was a bottle of clinic orange-juice leaking on the window-sill, oh it was disgusting. The house was quite horrid, and they were buying it on a mortgage, I can't think why – a horrid little terrace house, and you could even hear babies crying in the houses on either side. She said there were babies in every house. And at tea we had marge on the bread instead of butter, it was like the war. Bill was out at work. She tried so hard not to show me what she was feeling but poor thing, one could tell at a glance – she hadn't brushed her hair, or worn make-up for days, I shouldn't think, and she hadn't any stockings on although it was cold and she hadn't bothered to shave her legs, they were all blue and cold – she never took her apron off the whole time I was there. And in the end it all came out, I asked her something about Bill and she started to complain about him, she said that that kind of life was all right for him because at least he spent the day with intelligent people, and I said what intelligent people, and she said the other teachers at the Polytechnic, and when I said that I didn't think they could be much fun either she said anyway they were better than babies and the milkman. Oh God, I've never heard such abuse from anyone, she sounded like a fishwife or something off the music-halls, and all the time she was shovelling Farex down that poor little kid. And I said to myself as I left, never never never will I let that happen to me. Never will I marry without money.

'I suppose that what I really said to myself was, I will never have children. I want my life, I want it now, I don't want to give it to the next generation. So I took bloody good care that it shouldn't happen to me.'

'Would you and Stephen never have had children?' I asked. I felt subdued with horror.

'Never,' she said. 'Never.'

I was silent. I was silenced. Louise stared into the fire. She had stopped shivering and had started to cry. The tears rolled down her nose and she didn't make any effort to stop them. She frightened me: I hadn't seen her cry since she was ten.

'I never went to see her again,' she said, after a while. She said it in such a way that I knew she had been worrying about it, for a long time. And then, after another long pause, she said, 'Stella wrote to me, while I was in Paris. She was in hospital after the second baby, and this time it was a boy. She said it weighed seven pounds, and had black hair, and that the hospital let it stay with her at night, but that she missed the little girl who wasn't allowed in even at visiting-time, they don't allow children in maternity wards. I didn't know that, it seems ironic, really. She'd written to the *Spectator* about it. She said she was sorry she'd been cross the day I'd been to see her, but the baby had kept her up all night teething, and she and Bill had had a quarrel about whose turn it was to get up for the early feed. She said she felt better now the other one was born.'

'I'm glad,' I said.

'Yes. But I couldn't go to see her again, could I? So I stayed away. And which was true, in any case, the letter or what I saw?'

Looking at her crying, so pitiably and unapproachably there, I saw for her what I could never see for myself – that this impulse to seize on one moment as the whole, one aspect as the total view, one attitude as a revelation, is the impulse that confounds both her and me, that confounds and impels us. To force a unity from a quarrel, a high continuum from a sequence of defeats and petty disasters, to live on the level of the heart rather than the level of the slipping petticoat, this is what we spend our life on, and this is what wears us out. My attitude to the petticoat is firmer than hers, but I am exhausted nevertheless.

'How could I go and see her again?' she repeated. 'I stayed away. And look at me now. What shall I do now? Whatever shall I do?'

'I don't know,' I said. I didn't like her to ask me. It seemed a kind of incest, just to watch her cry, so unfamiliar was any true proximity.

'If I were you,' she said, 'I would marry Francis. I think you should marry Francis.'

'I think I probably will,' I said.

'But I don't know what on earth I shall do,' she said again.

As I sit here, typing this last page, Francis is on his way home. He is somewhere in the middle of the Atlantic on his way home to me, and I am waiting to see whether or not I have kept faith. I am waiting to take my life up again, not indeed where I left off, for I shall only find where it is when I try. But somewhere, and somewhere further on, moreover.

Gill is still at home, I think, but Tony rang me the other day to ask where she was, so I suppose he will be making overtures to her himself soon.

And as for Louise, well, what was there that could have happened? She's living with John at the moment but she refuses to marry him, despite his entreaties, and despite Stephen's determination to divorce her as soon as possible. She says she has learned her lesson, but I don't know what she means by that. Wilfred tells me that Stephen is writing another novel with Louise as villainess: I foresee a book about a woman who is destroyed by a fatal streak of vulgarity, manifested by an inability to resist shades of mauve, purple and lilac. The odd thing is that John has turned out to be deeply and devotedly in love with her: he loves her as much as Francis and I used to love each other before the boat sailed, which is my high-water-mark of passion. He loved her before the wedding, just as seriously, and was outraged when she treated it all as a dramatic joke. He wasn't enjoying it at all. I shan't suspect actors as much in the future: John seems to have behaved better than most people I know. She may even marry him in the end, if she can ever face the fact that he really is fond of her.

The oddest thing of all is that she seems to have forgiven me for existing. She's so nice to me now, so genuinely nice: she tells me all sorts of things. She even said once that in marrying Stephen she was trying to stop me overtaking her.

She also said that when Stephen went and caught them together in the bath, what upset her most was that she was wearing her bath-cap. To keep her hair dry. She said she would have started a scene if she had had her hair loose, but with a plastic hat on like that she felt so ridiculous that she couldn't.

She must at heart be quite fond of both John and me: of John, to have worn it, and of me, to have told it.